The Devil's Left Hand

On a scorching August day, Luis Bucca – the Mexican gunslinger known as the Devil's Left Hand – rides into the Texan cattle town of Faro's Creek and guns down six of Burke County's most prominent citizens.

Among the victims is rancher John Devine. When news of his murder breaks, his brother Will determines to hunt down Bucca and solve the mystery of why he should have shot six innocent men. Was he hired to do it? And if so, by whom and for what reason?

By chance, Devine's old friend Jack Stone rides into town and offers to help bring Bucca to justice. And famous gunfighter Stone is just the man to do just that!

The Devil's Left Hand

J. D. KINCAID

A Black Horse Western

ROBERT HALE · LONDON

ISBN-10: 0-7090-8117-0
ISBN-13: 978-0-7090-8117-3

Robert Hale Limited
Clerkenwell House
Clerkenwell Green
London EC1R 0HT

Typeset by
Derek Doyle & Associates, Shaw Heath
Printed and bound in Great Britain by
Antony Rowe Limited, Wiltshire

ONE

Luis Bucca rode slowly across the town limits and into the small, dusty Texas cattle town of Faro's Creek. It was high noon and a scorching August sun beat down upon the deserted main street. The Mexican scanned the buildings on either side and a gleam entered his cruel, coal-black eyes as he observed the Longhorn saloon. He urged his black mare forward, then reined her in when he drew level with the saloon. He dismounted and hitched the mare to the rail in front of the Longhorn.

Bucca was dressed in black from the top of his wide-brimmed sombrero to the tips of his shiny leather boots. Kerchief, shirt, vest and pants were a uniform sable, contributing to his undoubted aura of menace. Tall and lean, Bucca had a thin, gaunt face with high cheekbones, a sneering mouth and narrow jaw. But it was his cold, pitiless eyes that were inclined to inspire the most fear. Luis Bucca was quite clearly not a man to be crossed. He carried a Winchester in his saddle boot, a thin-bladed knife in a sheath at his waist and a single pearl-handled forty-five calibre British Tranter tied down on his left thigh. Like the notorious William Bonney, he was a left-handed gunman.

Slowly, deliberately, the Mexican climbed the flight of wooden steps leading up on to the stoop, and then he pushed open the batwing doors and walked into the saloon.

The bar-room was like a hundred others in towns across the West. Brass lamps hung from the rafters, the floor was sawdusted, there was a scattering of tables and chairs, and at the far end was the bar, with its hammered copper bar-top and, behind it, a large rectangular mirror. Ferdie Brownlee, the bartender, bald-headed, red-faced and pot-bellied in his rather grimy white apron, stood behind the bar, casually polishing glasses, for he had few customers.

There was nobody standing at the bar, the town drunk sprawled senseless across one of the tables, a couple of homesteaders sat at another table discussing the price of corn and, at a third table, half a dozen men were playing poker. These comprised the Longhorn saloon's entire clientele on that hot and humid afternoon. It was in the evenings when the saloon was busy.

The poker-school was a weekly affair. The same six met every Wednesday mid-morning and played through until late in the evening. The game rarely ended much before midnight and invariably the stakes were high, for the players were among the wealthiest men in Burke County. Nobody recalled quite how the tradition had begun, but all looked forward to it, for it was a welcome break in their otherwise busy working week.

The oldest man at the poker-table was Gus McKinley, the proprietor of the Longhorn saloon. He was a small, scrawny fellow, with a shock of shaggy white hair and a large, luxuriant, white moustache. He wore a black city-style suit with an emerald-green velvet vest. Since his Longhorn saloon was the only saloon in town and catered not only for the inhabitants of Faro's Creek, but also for the cowboys from the Double D and Happy Valley ranches, it earned McKinley a pretty good living. This was supplemented by his winnings at the weekly poker-game, for the saloonkeeper was the shrewdest and most adept of the six players and won rather more often than he lost.

On McKinley's right hand sat Bart Richards, the mayor of Faro's Creek. He owned the town's only hotel and was, in addition, the proprietor of the livery stables. A large, flamboyant character, Bart Richards was probably the worst poker-player at the table. Clad in a white linen jacket and brown breeches and sporting a large white Stetson, he invariably overplayed his hand. As a result, he rarely ended up a winner at the end of the day, although this did not seem to affect either his style of play or his eagerness to participate in the game each week.

Fred Cotton sat next to the mayor. He owned the general store and was a squat, ruddy-faced man with merry, twinkling, blue eyes behind his wire-framed spectacles. His grey city-style suit seemed one size too large and he wore his grey derby hat at a slightly rakish angle. Fred Cotton was a cautious, calculating kind of player.

None of the aforementioned three players carried a gun. Sam Bain did, however, an ancient Webley RIC revolver, which he had inherited from his father. A hardworking homesteader, Bain played an unpredictable and cunning game and, like the saloonkeeper, hardly ever left the table a loser. Spare and of medium height, with a weather-beaten face and horny hands, the homesteader donned his Sunday best for the occasion.

The last two players were both ranchers, the proud owners of the Happy Valley and Double D spreads. Lyle Moody was tall and lean, while John Devine was even taller and built like a bear. Both carried Remington revolvers tied down on their right thighs and both wore check shirts, denim pants, brown leather vests and brown leather boots. They differed, though, in their choice of headgear. Lyle Moody chose to wear a black, low-crowned Stetson. John Devine, on the other hand, sported a large, wide-brimmed grey hat.

All six men were so preoccupied with their game that they failed to notice Luis Bucca enter the saloon. He, for his part, strolled nonchalantly across the bar-room to the counter, where he caught the bartender's attention.

'A nice cold beer, if you please,' he said politely.

Ferdie Brownlee nodded, threw the towel, with which he had been polishing the glasses, over his shoulder and proceeded to pull the Mexican a beer.

'That'll be twenty cents,' he muttered.

'Thank you.'

Luis Bucca tossed a couple of dimes across the copper bar-top and picked up the glass of beer. He took a long draught and sighed contentedly.

'*Madre de Dios*, I needed that!' he declared.

Again the bartender nodded. The humidity had caused small beads of perspiration to break out on Ferdie Brownlee's brow.

Luis Bucca swivelled round to face the bar-room. He eyed the six men at the poker-table and carefully surveyed each player in turn. They were exactly as he had had them described to him. There could be no mistake; the poker-school was complete. Bucca smiled grimly. He knew what he had to do. The instructions given to him had been precise.

The poker-players, meantime, remained engrossed in their current game. Bart Richards had just dealt himself a flush in diamonds and Gus McKinley three eights, a king and a ten. The others had been rather less fortunate, Fred Cotton having been dealt a pair of tens, while Sam Bain had a pair of deuces, Lyle Moody an ace high and John Devine a hand the highest card of which was a jack.

All six were carefully studying their hand and deciding how to proceed when Luis Bucca made his move.

Leaving the half-finished beer at the bar counter, the Mexican stepped across the bar-room towards the poker-table. As he approached, Gus McKinley glanced up. He opened his mouth to ask the stranger if he wanted to join the game, but the words were never spoken, for, as he framed them, Luis Bucca suddenly whipped out his British Tranter and began shooting.

Bucca's first shot struck the saloonkeeper between the eyes and exploded out of the back of his skull in a cloud of blood and brains. His second took out the mayor's right eye, killing him instantly, and his third hit Fred Cotton in the chest, knocking him backwards out of his chair.

So swift and unexpected had been the attack that the three remaining poker-players had scarcely scrambled to their feet before Bucca's third victim hit the floorboards. All three went for their guns. But none was particularly adept with a gun and the man they were facing was a professional killer.

Luis Bucca cold-bloodedly gunned down each of

them in turn. Of the three, only John Devine succeeded in clearing leather, and he had barely done so before Bucca shot him through the heart. The Remington slipped from his nerveless fingers and clattered on to the floor, just as Bucca blasted the brains out of the heads of his two surviving companions.

Meantime, the two homesteaders were no longer discussing the price of corn, but had thrown themselves beneath their table, where they lay doggo, praying fervently that the Mexican wouldn't notice them. As for the town drunk, he had come to his senses, panicked and attempted to run. However, in his inebriated condition, he had managed only a couple of strides before he had stumbled and fallen. Now he lay spread-eagled across the floor, moaning softly.

The one other person remaining in the bar-room was also in a state of shock. Ferdie Brownlee stood for some moments, rooted to the spot, his normally ruddy complexion suddenly ashen. Then, all at once, his sense of self-preservation took control. The bartender turned and fled. There was a shotgun lodged behind the bar counter, but, such was Ferdie Brownlee's fear, he simply ignored it and, instead, ran straight through into the rear quarters of the saloon and from thence out of the back door.

Luis Bucca stood in the midst of the carnage he had created and proceeded to reload the British Tranter. Then he stared down in turn at each of his victims.

11

All except Fred Cotton were stone-dead. The store-keeper lay on his back with a huge, bloody hole in his chest. His eyes flickered and closed. Whether he would survive such a grievous wound was doubtful. Bucca watched the bloodstain slowly spread across the storekeeper's chest. He had his instructions. There were to be no survivors. He aimed his revolver at Fred Cotton's head and squeezed the trigger. All doubt was removed. He had fulfilled his contract.

Ignoring the two petrified homesteaders and the drunk, the Mexican recrossed the bar-room, pushed open the batwing doors and stepped out on to the stoop.

His shots had roused the townsfolk. Main Street was no longer deserted. A number of shopkeepers and householders had stepped out onto the side-walk. Others remained in their doorways or stuck their heads out of their windows. Only two men had summoned up enough courage to advance towards the Longhorn saloon. Marshal Jim Niven and his deputy, Larry Paulson, slowly, doggedly, made their way from the law office in the direction of the saloon.

Jim Niven was a tall, lean figure, with jet-black hair and whiskers and a distinctly lugubrious mien. He wore a black derby hat, white shirt and boot-lace tie, and a black three-piece city-style suit. And he carried an Army Model Colt in a holster on his right thigh. His deputy, a large, rather podgy young fellow in his early twenties, was similarly attired and he, too, carried an Army Model Colt. Both men looked and felt somewhat apprehensive. Shootings were rare in Faro's Creek. The most trouble the marshal and his deputy had to deal with was on Saturday nights when the cowboys from the Happy Valley and Double D ranches came to town. Then, they were occasionally called upon to break up some drunken bar-room brawl, but that was all.

The appearance of Luis Bucca on the stoop outside the Longhorn saloon did nothing to lessen the two lawmen's apprehension. Both recognized the Mexican from the Wanted poster pinned up in the law office.

'Hell!' muttered Niven. 'If'n that ain't Luis Bucca, who's known to one an' all as the Devil's Left Hand!'

'What in blue blazes is he doin' here in Faro's Creek?' cried Paulson.

'Shootin' folks by the sound of it,' replied the marshal.

'What folks?'

'Dunno, but I guess we're 'bout to find out.'

'Yeah.'

Luis Bucca halted at the top of the steps and stared hard at the approaching lawmen. They promptly stopped in their tracks. The distance between them and the Mexican assassin was approximately thirty feet.

'What in tarnation was that shootin' all about?'

demanded Jim Niven.

'I was simply fulfilling a contract,' replied Bucca coolly.

'A contract! What kinda contract?' cried the marshal.

Before Bucca could reply, Ferdie Brownlee ran out of the alley between the saloon and Fred Cotton's general store. As he sprinted past the two peace-officers and on up the street, he yelled, 'The sonofabitch has gunned down each an' every one of the Wednesday poker-school!'

'What?'

'In cold blood. They didn't stand a chance,' added the bartender, before hastily clambering up on to the opposite sidewalk and disappearing into the safety of the Faro's Creek Hotel.

'That is correct,' said Bucca.

'You . . . you've killed *all* of 'em?' exclaimed Niven.

'Luis Bucca does not shoot to wound. He shoots to kill,' replied the Mexican.

'Holy cow!'

'You . . . you realize you're talkin' to the law around here?' blustered Larry Paulson.

'I do.'

'Wa'al, you're under arrest. Ain't that so, Marshal?'

'It sure is,' said Niven, though he looked less confident than his words might have suggested.

Luis Bucca laughed a harsh, mirthless laugh.

'I do not think so,' he said coldly.

The two peace-officers stood for some moments, simply staring at the confessed assassin. Then, all at once, the deputy went for his gun. But he was much too slow. The Army Model Colt had barely cleared leather before Luis Bucca had drawn and fired his British Tranter. The forty-five calibre slug struck Larry Paulson in the chest and knocked him clean off his feet. He landed with a thud on his back in the dust of Main Street and lay quite still.

'Goddammit, you . . . you murderin' bastard, you've killed him!' exclaimed the marshal.

'And, if you should choose to go against me, I shall kill you, too,' said Bucca.

'Why you . . you. . . !'

'Take your revolver out of its holster and throw it behind you. Do this very slowly, Marshal, or I shall shoot you.'

Jim Niven gulped. He knew he ought to try to apprehend the Mexican, but he also knew that, if he did so, he would surely die. Slowly, reluctantly, he drew the gun from its holster and tossed it onto the ground behind him. It landed some fifteen to twenty feet from where he stood.

Bucca smiled and clattered down the short flight of wooden steps to the street. He dropped his revolver back into its holster and proceeded to unhitch the mare from the rail. Then, in one swift, fluid movement, he threw himself into the saddle.

15

'*Adios, señor!*' he cried and, digging his heels into the mare's flanks, he sent her galloping off along Main Street in the direction from which he had come. Immediately, Jim Niven ran to retrieve his gun, but the Mexican was out of range before he could raise it and take aim.

Those citizens who had been roused by the shootings watched Luis Bucca go. Nobody made any attempt to stop him. However, as soon as he reached the town limits and headed out on to the prairie, they bustled out of their doorways and hurried towards the Longhorn saloon.

The first to reach Marshal Jim Niven and his fallen deputy was Barnaby Jones the mortician, a thin, lugubrious-looking fellow in a black frock-coat and stovepipe hat, and Doc Saul Bailey, short, stocky and bespectacled and neatly attired in a smart black Prince Albert coat and derby hat. Close behind came the town's deputy mayor and local lawyer, Harvey Littlejohn He was a tall, dark-haired, broad-shouldered man, with a confident air and a handsome face, and his attire was similar to that of the marshal except that he wore a grey cravat in place of the other's bootlace tie.

Doc Bailey dropped down on to his knees beside the deputy marshal. He carefully examined him and then looked up. By now a small crowd had formed. The doctor shook his head.

'I'm afraid, Barnaby, that young Larry needs your

services rather than mine,' he said to the mortician.

Barnaby Jones nodded and removed his hat. Others in the crowd followed suit.

'OK, Marshal, jest what in blue blazes happened here?' demanded Harvey Littlejohn.

'You heard the earlier shots?'

' 'Course I did.'

'They came from inside the Longhorn saloon.'

'Yes?'

'That Mexican, he gunned down the entire Wednesday poker-school,' interjected the bartender, Ferdie Brownlee, from the edge of the crowd.

'Is that so, Marshal?' enquired Littlejohn.

'I guess it is. Ferdie should know. He was there,' said Niven.

'Wa'al, let's go take a look,' said the deputy mayor.

'We don't want everyone bargin' in. Not yet. Let's jest you, me, Ferdie an' the doc head on in. Oh, an' Barnaby can come along, too, jest as soon as he has made arrangements for Larry to be conveyed to the funeral parlour. The rest of you best stay out here.'

'Yeah, that seems sensible, Marshal,' agreed Littlejohn.

There were one or two mutterings, but the majority of the onlookers, shocked at the sight of Larry Paulson's corpse, were, in any case, none too eager to view the other six. They were quite content to remain outside.

The four men entered the saloon, Ferdie Brownlee bringing up the rear. They found that the two homesteaders and the town drunk had vanished, presumably having followed Ferdie Brownlee's example and fled out through the back door. Doc Bailey examined each body in turn.

'They're all dead,' he announced finally.

'So, tell us exactly what happened, Ferdie,' said Niven.

'Sure thing, Marshal.' The bartender proceeded to describe the events inside the saloon from the moment Luis Bucca walked in until the moment he walked out. 'I never saw nuthin' like it in my life,' he concluded.

'Who was he . . . the killer? Do you know, Marshal?' asked a white-faced Littlejohn.

'Yeah, I know,' said Niven. 'I recognized him from a Wanted poster. He's Luis Bucca, a professional assassin, known as the Devil's Left Hand.'

'The Devil's *Left* Hand?'

'Yeah, on account of he's left handed.'

'So, why would he wanta kill the entire poker-school, all six of 'em?' demanded Doc Bailey.

'Beats me,' said the marshal.

'It's plain crazy!' stated Littlejohn. 'It don't make any kind of sense. Who would hire him to do a thing like that?'

'Mebbe nobody hired him. Mebbe he jest did it. On the spur of the moment,' suggested Niven.

18

'He'd have to be plumb locco to gun down six total strangers for no good reason,' said Littlejohn.

'Wa'al, mebbe he is,' said Niven.

'Did he strike you as demented or out of control when you faced up to him?' enquired Doc Bailey.

'No, cain't say he did,' confessed Niven. 'He seemed pretty darned cool.'

'So, it is a mystery,' said Doc Bailey.

'Yeah, and it will remain so until he is apprehended and brought to justice. Then perhaps we shall learn what brought him to Faro's Creek and why he gunned down our six friends,' said Littlejohn. He turned to face the marshal and rasped, 'You didn't make much of an effort to arrest him.'

'No.'

'It was young Larry who tried to take him.'

'Yeah, an' he's dead.'

'What are you saying, Marshal?'

'I'm sayin' that I'd be dead, too, if'n I'd gone for my gun.'

'So, you're jest gonna let him git away?'

'No, I intend to form a posse an' pursue him. He could easily out-shoot me an' Larry, but he won't be able to out-shoot a dozen or more of us. There's safety in numbers, I reckon.'

'Wa'al, then, you'd best git started or Bucca will be back in Mexico 'fore you can hope to catch up with him.'

'If'n he's headed thataway.'

'That seems most likely. Have you any reason to suppose he's headed off somewhere else?'

'No, not really.'

'So?'

'Yeah, like you, I guess he'll be aimin' to cross back over the border.'

With these words Marshal Jim Niven turned and made for the door. He was closely followed by Harvey Littlejohn and the doctor, while the mortician, who had followed them in, and the bartender remained in the bar-room with the corpses of the six poker-players.

Niven stepped to the front of the stoop and addressed the waiting crowd, which had grown in numbers since he and the others had disappeared inside the Longhorn saloon.

'OK,' he yelled, 'the news is bad. As Ferdie told us, that sonofabitch of a Mexican gunned down six of our most prominent citizens as they attended their weekly poker-game. Wa'al, none of 'em has survived the shootin'.'

This revelation drew a collective gasp from the crowd.

'You gonna let that murderin' bastard git away with it?' cried the town blacksmith, Jake Fallon.

'No, Jake, I ain't,' replied Niven. 'I'm lookin' for a posse to mount up right here an' now, an' set off after him. You willin'?'

'Sure am!' affirmed the blacksmith.

'Who else is prepared to ride with me?'

'I am!'

'An' me.'

One after another, the townsfolk volunteered until there were fourteen ready to ride with the marshal. They were a mixed bunch, old and young, some from Faro's Creek itself and some from the homesteads surrounding the town.

Niven smiled. Luis Bucca might be the fastest gun this side of the Colorado River, but even he couldn't hope to outshoot fifteen of them. All they had to do was overtake the Mexican before he reached and crossed over the border. The question was, could they do that?

'OK, let's mount up an' ride out!' cried the marshal.

A certain amount of confusion followed, as the members of the posse fought their way out of the crowd and went in search of their horses. Nevertheless, ten minutes later they were all mounted and ready to go.

At their head, Marshal Jim Niven turned to face Harvey Littlejohn, who was now, since the demise of his friend, Bart Richards, the mayor of Faro's Creek.

'Good luck, Marshal! Good luck, men!' shouted Littlejohn.

Niven gave him a brief salute and then, with the posse at his back, he set off along Main Street in the direction taken by the murderous Mexican. The chase was on.

TWO

The scene was Sarah Rennie's rooming-house in East Street, on the outskirts of Burkeville, the capital of Burke County. It was late afternoon and Sarah had a gentleman caller.

Will Devine, a bachelor in his late thirties, had for some time been paying court to the lovely young widow. He had not so far asked her to marry him, but was slowly working up to doing so. It was barely a year since Bob Rennie had tragically been thrown from his horse and killed, and Will Devine sensed that the widow was not quite ready for remarriage.

They did, however, make a handsome couple. Will Devine was a tall, dark-haired fellow, with strong, regular features, a firm jaw and a ready smile. He was immaculate in a grey city-style suit, white shirt with ruffled collar and dark blue velvet vest. His black low-crowned, wide-brimmed Stetson adorned the widow's hatrack. Sarah, for her part, was a petite thirty-year-old blonde, the mother of a small son, and as pretty as a picture in her neat gingham gown.

They were drinking coffee and discussing Burkeville's forthcoming horse fair and the trade it would bring to the town. Will Devine owned one of the town's two hotels, a saloon, a feed-and-grain store and he also held the freehold of several of Burkeville's stores and shops. Although already a wealthy man, he was nevertheless happily anticipating the expected increased custom, while Sarah hoped to fill the few remaining empty rooms in her rooming house over the three days of the fair.

Their discussion was interrupted, however, by a loud knocking on the widow's front door.

'I'll git it,' offered Devine, and he rose and went to open the door.

When he did so, he found himself confronted by the short, stocky figure of Sheriff Donnie Dykes. The sheriff's usually jovial features were, on this occasion, wearing a solemn expression.

'I thought I'd find you here,' said Dykes.

'Wa'al, come in,' said Devine, and he led the lawman through into the widow's parlour.

'Oh, hullo, Sheriff!' exclaimed a surprised Sarah. 'To what do we owe the pleasure of this visit?'

'I'm afraid it ain't gonna be no pleasure,' replied Dykes.

'No?'

'No, ma'am. But it ain't you I'm here to see. It's Will I need to speak to.'

Will Devine gazed quizzically at the sheriff. He felt a sudden sense of foreboding.

'OK, spill the beans,' he said.

'I jest got a wire from Harvey Littlejohn in Faro's Creek.'

'He's the deppity mayor, right?'

'*Was* the deppity mayor. He's now the mayor. That's what he telegraphed me about. The mayor an' five others were gunned down as they played poker in the Longhorn saloon.'

'What day is it? Hell, it's Wednesday! That's the day of the regular poker-school, which my brother John attends!'

'Yeah,'

'Was John among the six gunned down, Donnie?'

'He was, Will.'

'Oh, my God!'

'I'm sorry.'

'How bad is it? Is he. . . ?'

'All six are dead.'

'Jeeze!'

Sarah went across and threw a comforting arm round Will Devine's shoulders. She glanced up at the sheriff.

'What happened? Who shot 'em an' why?' she demanded.

'According to Harvey Littlejohn's wire, they were

shot by one Luis Bucca, who escaped and is being pursued by a posse led by Marshal Niven,' said Dykes.

'Luis Bucca! Isn't he some kinda shootist?' enquired Devine.

'That's right, Will. He's known as the Devil's Left Hand an' is a hired gun, a professional killer.'

'But why would he kill that many folks?' cried Devine. 'I mean, who on earth would want all six of 'em dead?'

'It beats me,' confessed the sheriff.

'So, what are you gonna do?' asked Devine.

'Wa'al, I aim to co-ordinate a search across the length an' breadth of Burke County. I'm gonna wire every peace-officer in every township to git out lookin' for Bucca. Then I propose to ride over to Faro's Creek to observe the scene of the crime for myself.'

Devine sighed heavily.

'I'll ride with you,' he said.

'Fine. I'll do that there telegraphin' while you go git your hoss an' saddle up,' stated Dykes, adding, 'Meet me outside the law office.'

'OK.'

Devine escorted the lawman to the door and then returned to the parlour, where he took Sarah into his aims.

'I've gotta go,' he said, grim-faced.

'I know,' replied the widow.

'John an' I have always been close. Not all brothers git along, but we did.'

'Yes. You go, but be careful, Will. This Luis Bucca
sounds like he's a dangerous man.'

'I don't think he'll be lookin' for me.'

'No?'

'No, more likely he'll be ridin' hell for leather for
the Mexican border.'

'I s'pose.'

Sarah reached up and kissed Devine. They clung
together for some moments. Then he released her.

'I'll be back jest as soon as I can. But I'll need to
break the news to Chrissie an' family, an' then
there's the funeral to attend. Guess that'll be in
Faro's Creek.'

'Yes. Let me know when an' I'll come over.'

'Thanks, Sarah. I'd appreciate that.'

'Goodbye, Will.'

' 'Bye.'

Devine went to fetch his horse, a piebald, from
the livery stables. Sarah watched him go. Her heart
went out to him, for she knew how fond of his
brother he had been. As he disappeared into the
livery stables, she turned and closed the door
behind her. She had supper to prepare for her
lodgers.

It was some minutes before Will Devine emerged
from the stables and rode along Main Street to the
law office. Hitched to the rail outside was the sher-

iff's sorrel. Devine was still debating whether or not to dismount when Sheriff Donnie Dykes came out of the office.

'OK, Will, I'm ready to ride,' he said. 'I've sent wires to every marshal in Burke County an' I've also telegraphed the Mexican authorities.'

'You don't really expect Luis Bueca'll be taken 'fore he leaves Burke County, do you?'

'Nope. That's why I've wired Mexico.'

'If'n he makes it that far, I cain't see the Mexicans apprehending him. That's one helluva long border to patrol an' once Luis Ricca has crossed it he'll jest vanish for sure.'

'Yeah. Wa'al, mebbe when we git to Faro's Creek I'll send another wire, this time to the Texas Rangers' HQ in Austin.'

'That's a good idea. If anyone can catch that murderin' sonofabitch, it'll be the Texas Rangers.'

Sheriff Donnie Dykes made no comment. While he had no doubts about the Texas Rangers' capabilities, he doubted that anyone would stop the shootist from crossing into Mexico, if that was what Bucca was minded to do. Meantime, he was anxious to reach Faro's Creek and examine the scene of the crime. He mounted the sorrel.

'OK, Will, let's go,' he said.

They cantered out of Burkeville and along the trail that led to Faro's Creek, twenty miles away. It was likely to be a hot, dusty ride and, although both men were keen to reach their destination as soon as possible, neither intended to ride his horse into the ground. They contented themselves with a fast canter through the rugged hill country between the two towns.

Three miles outside the county seat they clattered round a bend in the trail and found themselves face to face with Marshal Jim Niven and his posse. They reined in their horses, as did Niven and his men. Once the dust had settled, the sheriff addressed the marshal.

'How's it goin', Jim?' he enquired.

'You know what we're about?' said Niven.

'Sure. Harvey Littlejohn telegraphed me an' I've notified every peace-officer in the county to look out for that murderin' Mexican, Bucca.'

'Wa'al, I dunno where he is. We headed south, but ain't seen hide nor hair of him. Now we're tryin' this here hill country in case he's holed up some place hereabouts.' Dykes smiled wryly. He was pretty sure that Luis Bucca was either well on his way out of the county or already gone.

'I wish you good luck, Marshal,' he said.

'Thanks. Where are you headed, Sheriff?' asked Niven.

'Faro's Creek. I wanta view the crime scene an' Will wants to see his brother.'

' 'Course.' Niven raised his hat. 'I'm mighty sorry 'bout John,' he said to the hotelier.

'Thank you, Marshal. It was a terrible shock. I guess Faro's Creek has seen nuthin' like it.'

'Yeah. Seven dead, includin' my deppity. I can still scarcely believe it.' Niven replaced his hat on his head. 'We gotta be goin'. Be seein' you at John's funeral,' he said.

Approximately one hour later, the two riders entered the town and rode down Main Street as far as the law office, where they dismounted and hitched their horses to the rail outside. The sheriff entered the office, intending to send off his tele-graph to the Texas Rangers before repairing to the Longhorn saloon. Will Devine, meanwhile, made his way along the sidewalk to the funeral parlour.

Inside, he was greeted by the mortician, Barnaby Jones.

'Afternoon, Will. I guess you've been told the sad news,' he said dolefully.

'Yeah.' Devine removed his low-crowned Stetson. 'May I see my brother?' he asked.

'Of course.'

Barnaby Jones slowly, sombrely, led the way through to a large rear room, where the six victims of the massacre and the dead deputy marshal were laid out. A huge table filled the centre of the cham-ber and the corpses lay side by side along its length. They remained clad in the clothes they had been wearing at the time of the shooting. Devine walked past the bodies of Bart Richards, Gus McKinley and

29

Fred Cotton and then halted beside that of his brother.

'May I have a few moments alone with John?' he murmured.

'Naturally. Stay as long as you like,' replied Barnaby Jones.

When the mortician had departed, Will Devine stretched out his arm and, bending low over his brother's body, took hold of the rancher's hand. He held it awhile, the tears coursing down his cheeks. He was not a man who cried easily, but, on this occasion, he made no attempt to restrain his tears.

John, the elder brother, had inherited the Double D ranch and Will, an independent spirit, had made his own way in the world rather than play second fiddle to his sibling. But that was not to say the brothers had not remained close. They had. The ranch was a mere ten miles outside Burkeville and Will had been a regular visitor. Now he felt an anguish and a despondency such as he had never before experienced, not even when his parents had died.

Eventually, Will Devine released his brother's hand, stood upright and wiped away the tears. Another emotion had entered his breast, that of anger. He determined there and then to hunt down his brother's killer if it was the last thing he did. But, before he could do that, there was the funeral to arrange and the news to break to John's widow,

Chrissie, and their two young sons. He was not looking forward to the former. The latter he was dreading.

It was with leaden steps that Will Devine returned to the outer office. Barnaby Jones was seated at his desk, attending to some paper work. He looked up as the hotelier entered and, rising, extended his hand.

'You have my most sincere condolences,' he said.

'Thanks, Barnaby.'

'I'll await your instructions regarding the funeral.'

'Yeah. I'll give you them jest as soon as I git back from breakin' the news to Chrissie.'

'A task I do not envy you.'

'No.'

'The Reverend Wanger has been informed and will presumably conduct all seven funeral services.'

'He's gonna be busy.'

'I'm afraid so.'

'As are you.'

'Yes.' Barnaby Jones reflected that Luis Bucca's visit had been good for business – his business, an unworthy thought, which he immediately expelled from his mind. 'I wish it weren't so,' he said.

'No. Wa'al, I'll be seein' you, Barnaby.'

'Yes. Please convey my condolences to Mrs Devine.'

'I will.'

Will Devine left the funeral parlour and had only just mounted his piebald when he was greeted by Donnie Dykes. The sheriff had viewed the scene of the crime and was now proposing to take a look at the victims.

'It still don't make no kinda sense,' said Dykes. 'I spoke to Harvey Littlejohn an' asked if'n Bucca had gone loco, but he didn't think so. Said Bucca seemed pretty much in control of hisself. Which points to his fulfillin' a contract.'

'A contract to gun down six fellers from quite different walks of life, who regularly, once a week, sit down to a game of poker? That's 'bout all they had in common.'

'Crazy, ain't it?

'Yeah.'

Will Devine turned the piebald's head and trotted off up Main Street. The Double D ranch lay a few miles to the east of the town and, once he had passed outside the town limits, Devine headed in that direction.

Donnie Dykes watched him go. He shook his head sadly. Since taking up the office of sheriff, there had been little crime in Burke County and he had coped easily. Now he felt distinctly out of his depth.

Meantime, Luis Bucca, the Devil's Left Hand, had left the county and was riding, not southwards towards the border with Mexico, but northwards. He had blood-money to collect.

THREE

At about the same time as Luis Bucca was murdering six innocent men in the Longhorn saloon, Frank Murphy, a professional gambler, was playing blackjack, some 250 miles north, in the Bucking Bronco. This saloon was situated in the small Kansas township of Lynx Crossing.

Lynx Crossing had sprung up as a cow town on account of its having a railroad. Many such towns, where the Texas cattle herds could ship off their beef at the end of a long cattle-drive, had emerged in recent times. Some had prospered while others had boomed for a year or two and then fallen into decline. Lynx Crossing was one that was fast declining, superseded by Wichita, five miles away. The trail herds no longer came and, consequently, the town had nothing to sustain it. Lynx Crossing was doomed.

Al Moody, the proprietor of the Bucking Bronco,

was well aware of the situation and had taken drastic steps to secure his future. For the moment, though, he was concentrating on dealing cards. All that morning's gamblers bar one had left the table poorer and probably no wiser. Only Frank Murphy still continued to play, and he was doing well. Very well. He was several hundred dollars the richer since entering the Bucking Bronco and sitting down at the table.

Al Moody scowled. He was not a happy man. Like his rancher brother, Lyle, he was tall and lean. He had thin, angular features and boasted a neat, pencil-thin moustache. His grey city-style suit was somewhat threadbare and it was evident he had seen better days. Indeed, he could ill afford to lose.

In contrast, Frank Murphy looked spruce and affluent in *his* immaculate grey suit, with its navy-blue brocade vest. A small, jaunty figure, Murphy wore his grey derby at a rakish angle and played his cards with the confidence of a gambler on a good run. Indeed, he had had many good runs over the years and had lived pretty well from the proceeds.

The average house advantage on blackjack was reckoned to be 5.6 per cent, yet it was a game in which the individual player's skill could overcome this. And Frank Murphy was an extremely skilful player. His strategy was to hit on a score of sixteen or lower if the dealer showed a seven or above, while standing on a score of twelve or higher if the dealer showed a six or lower. This simple strategy, he figured, reduced the house advantage to zero.

Certainly, at the Bucking Bronco's blackjack table the strategy had worked perfectly and, at ten minutes past noon, Frank Murphy decided it was time to play his last hand, win or lose. He had the feeling that the house was running low on ready cash and, besides, there was a high-roller's poker-game in Wichita that he had heard about, and he was eager to participate in it.

Murphy placed a wager of fifty dollars. He wanted to finish on a big bet. Al Moody's scowl deepened. He dealt two cards face up to the professional gambler, a ten of hearts and an eight of spades. Then he dealt himself a six of hearts and another card, face down.

'I'll stand,' said Murphy quietly.

Slowly, hesitantly, the saloonkeeper turned over his second card. It was a ten of clubs. Al Moody swore beneath his breath. He was forced to draw another card and the odds were that, should he do so, he would bust. He dealt himself the third card, a nine of diamonds.

'Goddammit!' he exploded.

'I win,' said Murphy.

'Yeah.' Al Moody reluctantly paid out. 'Another hand?' he muttered darkly.

Murphy shook his head.

'Nope, he said. 'I gotta be goin'.'

'You ain't gonna give me the chance to win some of my money back?' enquired Moody.

'Nope. You're the house. You got an advantage. If'n you cain't win with that, that's jest too bad.'

So saying, the gambler rose to his feet.

Al Moody sat grim-faced as Frank Murphy strolled across the bar-room and out through the batwing doors. Then, once Murphy had vanished outside, he beckoned to the three rough-looking characters who were drinking at the bar.

The Wilkins brothers had been hired by Moody during the town's brief boom when the cattlemen were still ending their drives at Lynx Crossing. Then he had needed the brothers to ensure that drunken cowpokes on the rampage didn't do too much damage to the Bucking Bronco. They had acted as his private law-enforcement team within the confines of the saloon. Should the cowboys cause trouble elsewhere in town, he was content to let Marshal Matt Cozens deal with it. Now, in the total absence of any cowboys, the brothers were no longer needed, but he was stuck with them.

Seth Wilkins was the eldest, a big bear of a man, heavily bearded, mean-eyed and vicious. Jake and Dan were both slightly smaller, but nevertheless tough, thickset fellows, and they, too, sported beards. Dan, the youngest, bore a livid scar from the corner of his left eye to the jawline. All three were clad in Stetsons, check shirts, leather vests, denim pants and boots, and each carried a Remington in his holster. Wanted for murder and robbery in no fewer than four different states, they had been content to hole up at Lynx Crossing.

'You want somethin', boss?' rasped Seth Wilkins.

'Yeah,' said Moody. 'I got a li'l job for you boys. I want you to follow that feller who jest finished playin' blackjack an' left.'

'He skin you, boss?' enquired Jake Wilkins.

'Yeah, he sure did.'

'For how much?' asked Dan Wilkins.

'Jest over five hundred bucks.'

'Jeeze!' Seth Wilkins whistled. 'That's one helluva loss!'

'You don't need to tell me that,' snapped Moody.

'No?'

'No, Seth. It's money I cain't afford to lose. Which is why I want you to follow the sonofabitch.'

'What have you got in mind?' Seth Wilkins grinned wickedly. 'As if I cain't guess,' he added.

'I want you to shoot him, dump him some place out in the desert where the buzzards an' coyotes will pick him clean, an' bring the money back here.'

Again Seth Wilkins grinned.

'S'pse we jest kill him an' ride off with the money?' he said.

'Lynx Crossing may be near bankrupt, but I ain't. I've taken some measures to make pretty darned sure I'll survive. 'Deed I reckon I'm gonna be rich,

37

but, in the meantime, jest in case things don't pan out, I need to git back those five hundred bucks. You git them for me an', if'n things *do* pan out, I'll make sure you boys earn some real money.'

'How?'

'I'll explain when you return.'

Seth Wilkins eyed the saloonkeeper closely. Was Al Moody telling the truth? Did he really have a plan to make himself rich, or was he simply saying that to ensure the brothers didn't ride off with Frank Murphy's winnings? There was no way of knowing, yet Seth Wilkins's instincts told him that the saloonkeeper was in fact telling the truth. Consequently, he determined to return to the Bucking Bronco with the $500. After all, should he discover that Al Moody was not about to become rich, he need not hand over the money.

'OK, boss,' he said. 'You got yourself a deal.' Then, turning to his two brothers, he rasped, 'Come on, boys, we got a job to do.'

The other two grinned.

'Sure thing, Seth,' said Jake Wilkins, while Dan chuckled and fingered the butt of his revolver.

Al Moody stepped outside on to the stoop and watched the three brothers mount and ride off. Since they were unsure as to which direction the gambler had taken, Seth Wilkins headed down Main Street and took the trail leading to Wichita, his brothers meantime galloping up Main Street and taking that which led to Dodge City.

Seth Wilkins rode hard and fast, spurring on his chestnut as he proceeded along the Wichita trail. He had approximately five miles in which to catch the gambler before he reached his destination. He prayed that Murphy was in no hurry to reach Wichita. If he was, then it was quite likely he would get there before Wilkins could overtake him.

In the event, the gambler was in no particular hurry and was loping along at an easy canter. He was some two miles outside Lynx Crossing when he became aware that somebody was galloping up behind him. Glancing over his shoulder, he spotted Wilkins riding hell for leather. Since he had been concentrating on the game of blackjack at the Bucking Bronco, he had barely given the brothers, who were drinking at the bar, a glance. Yet he was aware that there was something familiar about the man. And, as the other closed on him, he felt a sudden apprehension. He dug his heels into the flanks of his grey mare, but he was too late.

Seth Wilkins pulled a Winchester from his saddle boot and fired from the saddle. His first two shots passed harmlessly over Frank Murphy's head. The third, however, struck Murphy in the left shoulder and toppled him from his horse. He hit the ground in a cloud of dust and rolled off the trail into a tangle of mesquite. Scrambling into the cover of the dense shrub, Murphy crouched down and pulled his .30 calibre Colt from the shoulder-rig hidden beneath his grey jacket. This caused him some pain from his wound, which was bleeding profusely.

Meantime, Wilkins had dismounted, slipped the Winchester into his left hand and drawn his revolver from its holster. He dived into a tumble of boulders on the opposite side of the trail to the mesquite.

There followed a lull. Silence descended upon the trail, broken only by the cry of a lone buzzard wheeling high in the sky. Both men lay in their respective hideaways, pondering on what to do next.

Frank Murphy considered lying doggo until darkness fell and then slipping away and heading for Wichita, on foot if need be. His horse stood a good twenty yards away, munching the coarse tabosa grass that grew beside the trail, and the gambler realized that any attempt to reach and mount his grey mare would inevitably end in his being shot dead. But to do nothing for the next few hours was not a viable option either, for, should he do this, Murphy feared he would bleed to death. He urgently needed to reach town and have his wound tended.

Seth Wilkins was also in something of a quandary. He reckoned that, sooner or later, his two brothers would conclude that their quarry had headed in the opposite direction, and so would turn round and head back to Lynx Crossing. Thereupon, finding that he had not returned, they would surely set off in search of him. And, with his brothers to help him, Seth Wilkins figured he would have little trouble in flushing out the gambler from his refuge amongst the tangle of mesquite. But what if other folks should arrive upon the scene ahead of his brothers? After all, he was on the main trail leading to Wichita. Could he afford to wait and, consequently, chance that happening?

Wilkins decided that he could not wait. He had to flush out the gambler without delay. The question was, how would he manage to do it? He peered over the top of one of the boulders in front of him. As he did so, Frank Murphy fired his revolver. The .30 calibre bullet struck the rock and ricocheted past Wilkins's left ear. Immediately, Wilkins ducked down again. He had guessed that Murphy would be armed. Now he knew for certain that he was. Glancing about him, he suddenly noticed a shallow arroyo to his left. It was dry and snaked up the rocky hillside behind him.

Cautiously, Seth Wilkins crawled on his belly through the tumble of boulders and then slipped down into the arroyo. He was thankful it wasn't winter, otherwise the watercourse would be filled and crawling along it would be difficult if not impossible. As it was, he easily squirmed up the rock-strewn hill towards its summit.

From this prominence Wilkins reckoned he

would be able to look down upon the mesquite in which the gambler was lurking. And so it proved. While at ground level Wilkins's view of Frank Murphy was completely obscured by the tangle of shrub, from above there were gaps and he could see the crouching gambler quite clearly.

Wilkins raised the Winchester, clamped the butt to his shoulder and took careful aim. Then he fired. Once, twice, thrice the rifle barked. All three shots struck the wounded man. Murphy cried out, attempted to rise and promptly fell back, the third of Wilkins's shots having struck him between the eyes and blasted out his brains.

His killer waited for a minute or two. Then, certain that Murphy was not feigning, but was indeed dead, Wilkins scrambled to his feet and hurried back down the arroyo to the trail. He crossed over and fought his way through the mesquite to where the gambler lay dead. Crouching down, he searched the bloodied corpse for the $500 Murphy had won at the Bucking Bronco. Having found the money, Wilkins carefully stuck the wad of banknotes into the pocket of his brown leather vest. This done, he went across to where the gambler's grey mare stood grazing. He removed the saddle and bridle and sent the mare cantering off down the trail in the direction of Wichita. Then, he returned to the edge of the mesquite and hurled both saddle and bridle into the midst of it.

Seth Wilkins grinned and patted his vest pocket. He would return to Lynx Crossing and decide then whether or not to hand over the money to Al Moody. He mounted his horse and set off back along the trail towards the one-time cattle town.

His arrival in Lynx Crossing happily coincided with the return of his brothers. They had ridden hard and fast for several miles and, as he had expected they would, had eventually concluded that their quarry was headed in the opposite direction. Seth Wilkins quickly confirmed that their conclusion had been correct, and the three of them dismounted and trooped up on to the stoop and into the Bucking Bronco. The afternoon trade was quiet, for there were no gamblers and only a few drinkers.

The bartender was quietly polishing glasses and the saloon's only sporting woman was snoozing upstairs. Consequently Al Moody could afford to leave the bar-room. He beckoned the brothers to follow him into his office.

In the interim, while they had been pursuing the gambler, the saloonkeeper had received a wire from Harvey Littlejohn.

'I have had some bad news, boys,' he said.

'Yeah, boss?' Seth Wilkins eyed the saloonkeeper curiously.

'My brother Lyle has died.' Moody did not say that he had been shot dead. 'I shall be leaving immediately to arrange and attend his funeral,' he added.

'Right.'

'But, before I go, I'd like to know whether you succeeded in recovering the five hundred dollars I lost?'

'We did.' Seth Wilkins grinned. 'Or, to be exact, I did.'

'Good!'

Seth Wilkins produced the wad of banknotes, but did not hand them over.

'You said you had taken measures that were gonna make you rich,' he rasped.

'That's so.'

'Wa'al. . . ?'

'I'm gonna tend to that li'l business jest as soon as I've buried Lyle. Which means I may be gone some time.'

'Whereabouts exactly are you headin'?'

'Texas.'

'The Lone Star state. That's pretty big country.'

'Yeah' Al Moody smiled. 'You don't believe I'm gonna be rich, do you?' he asked.

'Nope.'

'You figure I'm gonna take those five hundred dollars an' ride outa here, never to return.'

'Wa'al, as you said yourself, this town is goin' bankrupt. In a few months it could be a ghost town.'

'Yup. But I got assets here, which I sure as hell

ain't aimin' to abandon. Once I've settled matters in Texas, I'll be back to clear up things here. An', jest to show you that I really have high expectations, I'm gonna let you keep the five hundred dollars.'

Seth Wilkins whistled softly, while his brothers looked agreeably surprised. Seth had been expecting to have some protests from Al Moody in the event of his proposing to hold on to the money. Now, unpredictably, the saloonkeeper was simply giving it away.

'That's mighty generous of you, boss,' he conceded.

'Not at all. You fellers have served me well,' said Moody.

'We aim to please, grinned Seth Wilkins. 'Don't we, boys?'

'Sure do,' said Jake Wilkins.

'That's right,' agreed Dan Wilkins

'Wa'al, I got one last li'l job for you,' said Moody.

'Oh, yeah?' said Seth Wilkins.

'Yeah. I jest received a telegram warnin' me that an ol' enemy was on his way to Lynx Crossing,' said the saloonkeeper. 'Got it an' the wire informin' me 'bout my brother Lyle's death within a few minutes of each other.'

'So, you headin' south to Texas for your brother's funeral is kinda opportune.'

'It is, Seth. I guess I won't be around when this feller gits here.' Moody shrugged his shoulders and added glumly, 'But I figure he'll await my return.'

'Who is this enemy of yourn?'

'A Mexican shootist named Luis Bucca.'

'Never heard of him,' growled Seth Wilkins. He turned to his brothers. 'Have either of you boys?'

'Nope,' said Jake Wilkins, while Dan merely shook his head.

'He's pretty darned notorious down Texas way,' said Moody. 'An' I don't want him hangin' around Lynx Crossing when I git back.'

'What are you sayin', boss?' enquired Seth Wilkins.

'I want him dead,' stated Moody.

'Ah!'

'I'm willin' to pay you one thousand dollars to shoot the sonofabitch.'

All three brothers gasped in amazement. Al Moody handing over the $500 had surprised them. This new offer astounded them.

'You sure must want this here Mexican shootist good an' dead if'n you're prepared to pay that kinda loot,' commented Seth Wilkins.

'I told you, I'm gonna be rich,' said Moody. 'When I return to settle things here, I wanta hear that Luis Bucca is dead. Then you'll git the thousand dollars. Don't worry, I won't have no trouble payin' you.'

Seth Wilkins considered the matter. He had to admit that Al Moody had been a good boss. Moody had paid a fair wage in the boom years *and* in recent times. He had made no attempt to claim back the $500 that Seth had retrieved from the late Frank Murphy. Now he was offering them $1,000 to gun down this Luis Bucca. The question was: would he return to pay this blood-money? Seth Wilkins thought about it and reckoned he would. Otherwise why should the saloonkeeper be bothered about the Mexican riding into and staying over in Lynx Crossing?

'OK, it's deal,' he said.

He glanced at his brothers. Both nodded their agreement. Neither was about to turn down the opportunity to earn the kind of money Al Moody was offering.

'It won't be easy money,' Moody warned him. 'Luis Bucca is a professional assassin.'

'We're gonna be three to one. We'll take him,' said Seth Wilkins confidently.

'Yeah, wa'al, don't underestimate him.'

'We won't.'

'OK. Now, I'd better describe what he looks like.'

'Hell, boss, we don't never git no Mexicans up here. This is Kansas, not Texas. He'll stand out like a sore thumb.'

'Even so. I sure don't want you gunnin' down the wrong feller. So, here goes. Bucca is tall an' lean, an' is likely to be dressed all in black. An' he carries a pearl-handled British Tranter tied down on his left

47

thigh. Also, last time I saw him, he was ridin' a coal-black mare.'

'We git the picture,' said Seth Wilkins.

'Wa'al, jest make certain that you git the man,' said Al Moody.

'When d'you reckon he'll arrive here in Lynx Crossing?'

'I don't know exactly. But it'll be within the next few days. I figure by Saturday at the latest.'

'OK. We'll keep a look-out for him.'

'You do that. An' I suggest you shoot him some place outa town. You don't want our marshal arrestin' you for murder.'

'Leave it to us, boss. When you return, I guarantee this Luis Bucca will be dead an' buried an' nobody any the wiser.'

Al Moody grinned. That was exactly what he wanted to hear.

'Right, Seth. I'll leave it to you an' your brothers,' he said.

Seth Wilkins smiled and asked, 'When roughly can we expect you to return an' settle up?'

'Like I said, I may be gone some time. A coupla weeks, perhaps longer. But I'll be back, an' then we'll have ourselves a celebration. I promise you that.'

Seth Wilkins and his brothers grinned broadly. They no longer cared if and when Lynx Crossing declined into a ghost town. With the $500 already in the bag and the promise of $1,000 more to come, they intended to celebrate with Al Moody and then head for the hot spots of either 'Frisco or Chicago.

'OK, boys, let's drink to the memory of my dear departed brother an' to our future prosperity,' suggested Moody.

The three brothers happily acquiesced and, several beers later, a not entirely sober Al Moody set out on the trail south towards Texas.

Then, following the departure of Al Moody, the three Wilkins brothers held a council of war. They sat round the abandoned poker-table and planned how they would get rid of Luis Bucca. There were still few drinkers in the saloon, although by now the Bucking Bronco's sole sporting woman had put in an appearance. Scarlett Duval was a pretty, plump, blonde thirty-year-old who enjoyed her work. Her bright-blue eyes twinkled merrily and her inviting red lips were parted in a saucy grin, as she chatted to one of the drinkers at the bar. He, for his part, could hardly take his eyes off the blonde's ripe white breasts, which threatened at any moment to pop out of her low-cut scarlet dress. Neither she nor he, nor any of the other drinkers, could overhear the brothers' discussion since the poker-table stood some distance from the bar and, in any case, they took good care to keep their voices low.

'OK,' said Seth Wilkins, 'I guess we better plan things carefully. Accordin' to the boss, this Luis

Bucca is a professional shootist, so we cain't take no chances.'

'We're gonna be three to one,' commented Jake.

'Two to one,' Seth corrected him.

'Whaddya mean? There's. . . .'

'I figure that you an' me can take the Mexican.'

'What about me?' demanded the youngest brother, Dan.

'We need someone to stay behind an' mind the store or, in this case, the saloon.'

'So, we ain't gonna wait for him here?' said Dan.

'The boss said we should shoot the sonofabitch some way outa town.'

'Yeah, so he did,' growled Jake.

'Wa'al,' said Seth, 'I reckon Buzzard Gulch is the perfect spot for an ambush. It's a coupla miles off an' on the main trail, an' Luis Bucca is darned near certain to ride through it on his way into town.'

The others thought about this for a moment or two.

'Yeah,' said Jake finally. 'We can pick him off real easy there. He'll be a sittin' duck.'

'That's what I figured,' grinned Seth. He stroked his beard and turned to his youngest brother. 'You OK 'bout bein' left behind in charge of this here saloon?' he enquired.

Dan nodded.

'I s'pose,' he said, then laughed harshly and added, 'though I guess you two are gonna have all the fun. Hell, I didn't even git to take a shot at that gambler!'

'Neither did I,' growled Jake. 'But, Seth, mebbe we could take Dan along an' leave Joey in charge here?' He indicated the bartender with a jerk of his thumb.

Seth glanced across at the man behind the solid mahogany bar counter and slowly shook his shaggy head.

'Nope,' he said. 'Joey has his hands full jest dispensin' drinks. If there was to be any trouble, I doubt he'd be able to handle it.'

'Yeah, guess you're right,' said Jake. 'Sorry, Dan.'

'Next time there's any killin' to do, I guarantee we won't leave you out,' promised Seth, with a conciliatory grin.

Dan smiled wryly.

'OK,' he said. 'So, when are you boys aimin' to head for Buzzard Gulch?'

'The boss didn't seem to know when the Mexican was gonna hit town. He said Saturday at the latest, so I figure he wasn't expectin' him to arrive as early as today.' Seth again stroked his beard and then, after some moments' consideration, declared, 'Jake an' me will pick up some provisions tomorrow mornin' an' head on out there.'

'You reckonin' on campin' somewhere in the gulch till this here Mexican turns up?'

'That's right, Dan.' Seth glanced at his other

51

brother. 'That OK with you, Jake?' he asked.

'Guess so, Seth. We sure as hell don't wanta mess up on this. Not with one thousand dollars ridin' on it.'

'No.'

All three grinned broadly. The prospect of all that money, and the fun they would have spending it, had put them in the best of spirits. They rose from the poker-table and sauntered back across to the bar, where Seth Wilkins ordered three large whiskeys. Then he produced from his vest pocket three cigars and handed one to each of his brothers.

Scarlett Duval watched then light up and take their first puff.

'You boys celebratin' somethin'?' she enquired perceptively.

Seth Wilkins leered at the blonde.

'Not yet,' he said, 'but we're shortly expectin' to.'

'An' jest what exactly are you gonna be celebratin'?'

'That'd be tellin'.'

'Which is why I'm askin'.'

Seth Wilkins tapped his nose and winked.

'We're expectin' to earn us some real money,' he said. 'An' when we do, the first thing I aim to do, by way of celebratin', is to tumble you.'

Scarlett smiled her professional smile.

'Why wait that long?' she enquired provocatively.

Seth pondered on this suggestion. He lifted the whiskey, which Joey had placed in front of him on the bar counter, and threw it back in one gulp. Then he grabbed the blonde by the arm.

'OK, Scarlett,' he said, 'let's go upstairs an' have us some fun, for I'm suddenly feelin' kinda horny.'

'You can pay?' asked the blonde.

' 'Course I can pay.'

'Hey, jest a minute,' said the man with whom Scarlett had previously been chatting. 'I thought that we. . . .'

'Later, buddy, later,' said Scarlett.

The man looked for a moment as though he were going to continue his protest, but, after glancing at the formidable figure of Seth Wilkins, he thought better of it.

'Er . . . OK,' he agreed lamely.

Scarlett smiled and she and the eldest of the three Wilkins brothers slowly made their way upstairs.

Jake and Dan watched them go and then turned and downed their whiskeys.

'Another?' suggested Jake.

'Yeah. Why not?' said Dan amiably.

FOUR

It was early evening on the same day when Jack Stone rode his bay gelding into Faro's Creek. Tall and wide-shouldered, with grey-flecked brown hair and a rugged, square-cut face, and wearing a grey Stetson, a red kerchief, a grey shirt beneath his knee-length buckskin jacket and blue denim pants, the Kentuckian looked and was a pretty tough *hombre*. He carried a Frontier Model Colt in his holster and a Winchester in his saddle boot, and his skill with both had on many occasions saved his life.

His had been an eventful thirty-odd years, during which he had lost a wife in childbirth, survived the Civil War, served as an Army scout, been a sheriff and a deputy US marshal, and achieved fame as the man who tamed Mallory, the roughest, toughest town in the state of Colorado. Forever a rover since the death of his beloved wife, Stone was presently looking up a couple of old friends from his cattle-driving days.

The Kentuckian's cool blue eyes scanned the building on either side of Main Street. He was looking for the law office. And, upon finding it, he dismounted, hitched the gelding to the rail outside, clambered up on to the sidewalk and stepped inside. Since Marshal Jim Niven was still out scouring the hills for Luis Bucca, the Kentuckian found the law office deserted.

'Lookin' for the marshal, mister?'

Stone turned to find himself confronting Sheriff Donnie Dykes, who was standing in the doorway.

'Are you him?' asked Stone.

Dykes shook his head.

'Nope. I'm the county sheriff.'

'Wa'al, mebbe you can help?'

'That's what I figured when I observed you enter this here office. Which is why I moseyed on over. So, what can I do for you?'

'I'm lookin' for the Double D ranch. I'm told it's only a few miles outside Faro's Creek. Mebbe you can give me directions?'

The sheriff's eyes narrowed.

'An' jest why would you be headin' there, stranger?' he enquired suspiciously.

'I'm lookin' for a coupla of pardners of mine, John an' Will Devine. I b'lieve they run that spread,' replied Stone.

'Will packed in some time back. His business interests are in Burkeville. John continued to run the ranch, though, till earlier this afternoon, when he was shot an' killed.'

'Holy cow!'

'Yeah, his death has shocked everyone. I informed Will an he's ridden over to the Double D to break the news to the widow.'

'How'd it happen? Was there a quarrel or somethin'?'

'Nope. It was the darnedest thing,' said the sheriff, and he went on to tell Stone of the massacre in the Longhorn saloon.

When Dykes had finished, the Kentuckian whistled softly and growled, 'But why in tarnation would this Luis Bucca gun down six total strangers? I mean, he's a professional assassin an' might have had a contract to assassinate *one* of them poker-' players. But all six of 'em. . . !'

'I know. I've been tryin' to make some sense of it, but cain't,' said Dykes.

'So, what steps have you taken to pursue an' arrest the murderin' sonofabitch?'

'I've alerted every peace-officer in Burke County, also the Mexican authorities an' the Texas Rangers.'

'You figure he'll be headin' for the border?'

'I do. 'Deed, I expect he's gone from this here county by now.'

'Hmm. Wa'al, guess I'll ride over to the Double

D. If'n you'll give me directions, Sheriff?'

'I'll do better'n that,' declared Dykes. 'I'll ride with you. Mebbe, between you, me an' Will, we can solve the mystery of why Luis Bucca claimed so many victims?'

'Yeah. It's sure a puzzle,' said Stone.

He extended his hand and, as Dykes grasped it, the sheriff said, 'Donnie Dykes. You have a name?'

'Stone. Jack Stone.'

The sheriff smiled.

'I've heard 'bout you, Mr Stone. You got yourself quite a reputation.'

'Guess so,' replied Stone wryly.

The two men left the law office, mounted their horses and set off down Main Street. The town remained in a state of shock. Small groups of people congregated along the sidewalks, discussing the horrific killing of so many of their prominent citizens. Among them was Harvey Littlejohn, the new mayor of Faro's Creek. He acknowledged the sheriff riding by with a solemn wave. Donnie Dykes raised his hat in reply and continued on towards the town limits.

Once beyond these limits, Dykes and the Kentuckian urged their horses from a canter into a gallop. The trail split in front of them and they took the left-hand spur. This led to the Double D ranch, five miles away. Both men were anxious to meet up with Will Devine and discuss with him what should be done to bring Luis Bucca to justice. On the other hand, neither was at all anxious to confront the grieving widow and her two young sons. That, however, was something that had to be faced.

In the event, Chrissie Devine and her two sons, John Junior and Jeff, were remarkably composed. That all three had been tearful and remained shocked and distressed was evident from the looks on their faces. Pale-faced and with red-rimmed eyes and grief-stricken countenances, they greeted the sheriff and the Kentuckian. They remained calm and in control of themselves, though, and, having received Dykes's and Stone's condolences, Chrissie was recovered enough to think to offer the two men coffee.

'Thank you, ma'am,' said Stone.

'Yes, thank you, Chrissie,' added the sheriff.

While Chrissie busied herself brewing the coffee, Stone turned to Will Devine.

'A terrible business, Will,' he said.

'Yes,' said Devine and, eyes glinting angrily, he continued, 'I vow here an' now I shall avenge John's murder. That murderin' bastard, Luis Bucca, ain't gonna git away with this, I tell you!'

'No,' said Stone. 'But I figure it ain't jest the Mexican who's responsible for the murder.'

'Whaddya mean?'

'Luis Bucca is a hired gun. The question is, who hired him?'

'To shoot down six innocent men! Six! What possible reason could anyone have to hire him to do that?'

'That's what I've been askin' myself,' muttered Dykes.

'It don't make sense. No, he jest did it for the sheer pleasure of killin'.'

'You're sayin' he went loco, Will?'

'Yup.'

'That ain't what Harvey Littlejohn thinks,' commented Dykes. 'Harvey reckons the Mexican seemed pretty cool when he left the Longhorn an' confronted Marshal Niven an' his deppity.'

'He also gunned down the deppity,' said Chrissie Devine sadly, as she handed mugs of hot, steaming coffee to the sheriff and the Kentuckian.

'Is that so?' said Stone.

'It is,' affirmed Dykes. 'Larry made the mistake of tryin' to out-draw Bucca.'

'An' the marshal?'

'Seems he figured discretion was the better part of valour.'

'He let Bucca escape?'

'Yeah. But don't condemn him, Mr Stone. Jim Niven ain't in Bucca's class as a gunfighter. He'd sure as hell have suffered the same fate as young Larry if'n he'd gone up against the Mexican.'

'An' jest where is the brave marshal now?' demanded Chrissie.

'He's leadin' a posse in pursuit of John's killer,' replied Dykes.

'You think they'll catch him?' she asked.

The sheriff shook his head.

'I doubt it. Bucca's probably well on his way to Mexico by now.'

'Mebbe, mebbe not,' said Stone.

'You figure there's some doubt 'bout where he's headed?' enquired Will Devine, a puzzled frown creasing his brow.

'I do,' said Stone.

'Why?' snapped the widow.

'Wa'al, we agree that Luis Bucca is a hired killer, right?'

'Right.'

'An' that someone's hired him on this occasion?'

'Yes, I reckon so.'

'OK. I dunno how it works, but my guess is that Bucca got part of his blood-money up front, with the rest to be paid once the deed was done.'

'That's the usual deal,' agreed Dykes.

'So, he'll be off now to collect the balance,' said Stone.

'Which means he may not necessarily be headin' for the border!' exclaimed Chrissie.

'Exactly. Bucca will be makin' for wherever the feller who hired him is hangin' out,' said the Kentuckian.

Sheriff Donnie Dykes nodded.

'I do believe you're right, Mr Stone,' he remarked.

'An' me,' averred Will Devine.

'OK,' said Stone. 'Therefore, what we've gotta do, is find out who's behind those killin's.'

'But how in tarnation do we do that?' cried Will Devine.

'There were six victims,' said Stone.

'Yeah.'

'Somebody wanted 'em dead. We need to discover why. So, firstly, what had they all in common?'

'They were all prominent men in Burke County,' stated Dykes.

'Wealthy men?'

'Yes, Mr Stone, pretty well off.'

'Wa'al, let me quote you from the Bible: *The love of money is the root of all evil.*'

'That's mebbe so, but if'n you think someone was expectin' to profit from those six deaths, you got it wrong,' said Will Devine. 'Sure, Chrissie here inherits the Double D ranch from John, but she don't inherit nuthin' from any of the others Bucca gunned down. An' the same applies to all the rest of the deceaseds' heirs. No one person can possibly profit from all six deaths.'

'No.'

'So, where does that leave us?' asked Dykes.

'There's somethin' else all six had in common,' said Stone.

'An' what's that?' growled the sheriff.

61

'They were all poker-players.'

'That's true. They played together each week on a Wednesday.'

'A tradition?'

'Yeah. Cain't remember when it began. Can you, Will?'

Devine shook his head.

'It's been goin' on a few years now,' volunteered Chrissie.

'So, whoever hired Bucca would likely have known about it?' mused Stone.

'Reckon,' said Dykes.

Stone smiled grimly. He had figured it out.

'Bucca's employer expected to profit from the death of only one of them poker-players,' he stated.

'Only one?' muttered Dykes.

'Yup.'

'Then why, in blue blazes, murder all of 'em?'

'In order to conceal his identity. Ain't that right, Mr Stone?' interjected Chrissie. Will Devine gazed at his sister-in-law in surprise.

'I do b'lieve you've hit on it, Chrissie,' he declared.

'Mr Stone hit on it,' Chrissie corrected him.

'Yeah, if the sonofabitch had hired Bucca to kill jest the one of 'em, it would have been kinda obvious who was behind the killin',' said Sheriff Donnie Dykes thoughtfully.

'It still would've been hard to prove, though,' said Will Devine.

'Mebbe. Anyway, Bucca's employer evidently wasn't prepared to take that chance,' said Dykes.

'No,' growled Stone. He had come up against all sorts of villains in his time, yet none more callous and greedy than the person who had planned this crime. To order the murder of five innocent men, simply to profit from the death of the sixth, was unforgivable. 'We gotta bring the bastard to book,' he rasped.

'Yeah, we cain't let the feller, whoever he is, git away with it,' agreed Devine.

'If it is a feller,' said Stone.

'Surely no woman. . . .' began Chrissie, and then she lapsed into silence.

'Wa'al, let's figure it out,' said Dykes.

'How?' asked Chrissie.

'What we need to know is who the next of kin are. One of 'em has gotta be the person who hired Luis Bucca.' Dykes scratched his head. 'Harvey Littlejohn wired me to tell you, Will, 'bout your brother. I reckon, as the only lawyer in Faro's Creek, he'll be the man to ask. Probably holds the wills of all six of 'em,' he added.

'He acted for John, certainly,' confirmed Chrissie.

'Then we'd best head back to Faro's Creek an' speak to him,' said Dykes.

'I'll ride with you,' declared Will Devine.

'An' me,' said Stone.

Will Devine stared hard at the Kentuckian.

'You sure you wanta git involved in all this, Jack?' he enquired.

'John was my friend,' said Stone. 'I am involved.'

'OK. Let's ride,' said Dykes.

The three men took their leave of Chrissie and her two sons and set off along the trail to Faro's Creek. As they passed through the gateway of the Double D they broke into a gallop. All three were anxious to interview the lawyer and, with luck, determine who was Luis Bucca's mysterious and murderous employer.

On entering Faro's Creek they reduced their speed to a fast trot and proceeded along Main Street in the direction of the lawyer's office. After dismounting and entering they found Harvey Littlejohn seated behind his desk, working through a stack of legal papers. The recent deaths had generated a deal of extra work for the lawyer, which was why he was working late.

Littlejohn looked pale and shaken, his usual urbanity for the moment shattered by what he had witnessed. Violent deaths were rare in Faro's Creek and certainly nothing like the massacre at the Lcnghorn saloon had ever before occurred in the town. He looked up at his visitors and smiled wanly.

'What can I do for you, gentlemen?' he enquired.

Donnie Dykes smiled back.

'We've come about yesterday's massacre,' he said. 'An' this, by the way, is Mr Jack Stone,' he added by way of introduction.

'Howdy,' said the Kentuckian.

'Good evening, Mr Stone,' said Littlejohn and then, staring curiously at the peace-officer, he repeated, 'What can I do for you?'

'We wanta know the next of kin of all those gunned down inside the Longhorn,' said Dykes.

'To what purpose?'

'We need to know who benefited from their deaths.' Dykes frowned and went on, 'We figure one of them there next of kin hired Luis Bucca to kill all six, reckonin' it would then make it darned near impossible for anyone to tell who'd hired him. You see, if'n he had shot only one. . . .'

'OK, I take your point,' said the lawyer.

'So, you'll help us?' enquired Stone.

'I will,' declared Littlejohn. 'I can list the next of kin, but that may not take you any further.'

'No, mebbe not. We'll have to see.'

'Wa'al, of course there's your sister-in-law, Will,' began Littlejohn.

'I think we can discount Chrissie,' said Devine.

'Me, too. So, let's move on,' said Dykes.

The lawyer nodded.

'Very well,' he said. 'I'll start with Gus McKinley then. His only relative, as far as I am aware, is a certain Nathaniel McKinley, a nephew. He is on his way here from Chicago, where he practises, like myself, as a lawyer.'

'The Longhorn saloon is worth quite a lot of loot,' commented Devine.

'So is Mr Nathaniel McKinley,' said Littlejohn.

'You know this for a fact?'

'I do, Will. I have had several dealings over the years with the firm of Brown, McKinley and Graham, of which Mr McKinley is a partner. They are both highly reputable and highly successful.'

' 'Sides, if'n he hails from Chicago, he'd surely have hired some hoodlum from that city to do his killin' for him.' Stone paused and then added wryly, 'Luis Bucca is pretty darned famous south of the Missouri, but I don't reckon anyone in Chicago will ever have heard of him.'

'So, we can discount Gus McKinley's nephew?' remarked Devine.

'I guess so,' said Stone.

'Next, Harvey, if you please,' said Dykes.

'Bart Richards, my predecessor as mayor, leaves a widow an' four children,' said Littlejohn.

'Sophie ain't any more likely than Chrissie to have planned the death of her husband,' stated the sheriff.

'I agree,' affirmed Devine. 'A devoted wife an' mother. So, Harvey, press on.'

The lawyer nodded.

'Fred Cotton similarly leaves a widow.'

'With six children,' added Devine.

'I cain't imagine Jane Cotton schemin' to git rid of Fred,' commented Littlejohn.

'Nor me,' said Devine. 'Not a homely, easy-goin' woman like Jane. It ain't credible.'

'Which brings us to Sam Bain,' said Littlejohn. 'A widower with but one child, his daughter Lizzie.'

'Who's married to Luke Drummond, one of the wealthiest ranchers in all Texas,' stated Sheriff Donnie Dykes.

'Yeah, his spread in Wyatt County is bigger'n the Double D an' Happy Valley spreads put together,' said Littlejohn. 'Why in tarnation would he or Lizzie want Sam's homestead?'

'They wouldn't,' declared Dykes firmly. 'Leastways, not enough to kill for it.'

'So, we come to the last of the six, Lyle Moody,' said Littlejohn, adding thoughtfully, 'Now his Happy Valley spread is worth killin' for.'

'Yeah, John always reckoned Lyle had even better grazin' than he did on the Double D,' commented Devine.

'An' the Double D is a pretty fine spread,' said Dykes.

'Sure is, Donnie.'

'Therefore, Will, mebbe Lyle's successor is our man. Lyle was a bachelor with jest the one brother. Ain't that right, Harvey?'

The lawyer nodded.

'Yes. I recall Al Moody only too well,' he said. 'A real ne'er-do-well, that one. Always gittin' hisself into trouble, a mean sonofabitch.'

'I remember. Whatever became of him?' asked Devine.

'After his last spell in jail, he lammed it outa Burke County. Headed north,' said Dykes.

'That's right,' said Littlejohn. 'Normally, I wouldn't divulge a client's business details, but in these circumstances—'

'Go on, Harvey,' urged the sheriff.

'Al Moody found hisself up in Kansas, in the small cattle town of Lynx Crossing, where it seemed that the town's one saloon was up for sale. Al wired his brother, askin' Lyle to bankroll him. Lyle wasn't keen, but he figured that if Al had a business to tend, mebbe he'd keep outa trouble. So, he agreed. I acted for him in this matter an' Al Moody got his saloon, the Buckin' Bronco, as I recall.'

'An' is Al still the owner of the Buckin' Bronco?'

'As far as I am aware, Donnie.'

'A number of them Kansas cattle towns have boomed an' bust,' interjected Stone. 'If'n Lynx Crossing is one that's gone bust. . . .'

'That would give Al Moody reason to plot his brother's death,' Sheriff Donnie Dykes finished the Kentuckian's sentence for him.

'An', as I remember Al, he's jest cunnin' an'

mean-minded enough to have devised that diabolical plan in order to divert suspicion,' said Littlejohn.

'But did he know about the regular Wednesday poker-game?' enquired Stone.

'Undoubtedly,' said the lawyer. 'The Wednesday poker-game had been established some time 'fore he left town. 'Deed, he wanted to join, but Lyle an' the others wouldn't let him. On account of that, when eventually Al left town, he an' Lyle parted rather less than amicably.'

'Yet he still came to his brother when he needed the money to purchase that saloon,' said Devine.

'That's Al Moody for you!' exclaimed Dykes.

'Which seems to make him our prime suspect,' added Littlejohn.

'Wa'al, it's one thing to suspect the sonofabitch,' said Devine. 'But it's quite another to prove he's the one who hired Luis Bucca.'

'I don't see how you're gonna prove it,' remarked the lawyer.

'No?'

'No, Will, I surely don't.'

'If we could catch the Mexican, mebbe he'd talk?'

'Mebbe, but first you gotta catch him,' said Stone. 'An' that ain't gonna be easy.'

'If Al Moody hired Bucca, then, as you said earlier, Jack, Bucca is likely on his way to collect the balance of his blood-money,' commented Devine.

'You reckon that Al Moody will wait in Lynx Crossing an' settle with the Mexican 'fore he heads down here to attend Lyle's funeral an' take over the ranch?' asked the Kentuckian.

'I do,' said Devine.

'I agree,' stated Sheriff Donnie Dykes.

'Then, I guess we'd best head north for Kansas,' said Stone.

'We, Jack?' cried a surprised Will Devine.

'I already said I was involved, John an' you bein' my friends.'

'But this could be dangerous. If we find Luis Bucca. . . .'

'You ain't no gunfighter, Will. I am. So, you're gonna need me along.'

'That's right,' said Dykes. 'An' I cain't ride with you. My place is here in Burke County. As sheriff, I got duties to attend to.'

'Luis Bucca's gonna have quite a start on you,' remarked Littlejohn. 'By the time you reach Lynx Crossing, he an' Al Moody will probably have concluded their business. He could well be long gone an' Al already on his way south.'

'Then we'll mebbe meet Al on the trail,' said Devine.

'Mebbe, though it's jest as likely you'll miss each other. There's more'n one trail,' said Dykes.

'Are you sayin' we shouldn't ride north to Lynx Crossing?' asked Stone.

'I'm simply sayin' it could well be a wasted journey,' said the sheriff.

'Exactly,' concurred the lawyer.

Devine glanced anxiously at Stone.

'Wa'al, whaddya think, Jack?' he enquired.

'I think we gotta go,' said the Kentuckian. 'There is, after all, jest a slim chance that we'll catch 'em together. If we don't, I cain't see how you're gonna prove Al Moody's involvement in them there killin's.'

Sheriff Donnie Dykes gave Stone's proposition a few moments' careful consideration.

'Yeah,' he said eventually, 'I guess it's our only chance of convictin' Al Moody of complicity in murder. An' if, at the same time, you can bring in the Devil's Left Hand. . . .'

Stone smiled grimly.

'We'll do our best, won't we, Will?'

'Sure will, Jack.'

'You are quite convinced, then, that Al Moody is the man behind the Longhorn saloon massacre?' said Littlejohn.

The other three glanced enquiringly at each other. Then they turned and addressed the lawyer.

'We are,' they declared in unison.

'In that case, I wish you success,' said Littlejohn.

'Thank you.' Stone smiled at Devine. 'Shall we ride?' he asked.

'Yup. Let's go, Jack,' said the other.

And so it was that, although darkness was beginning to fall, the two men set off on the long ride north. Before leaving the lawyer's office, Will Devine had asked the sheriff to call again on his sister-in-law and ask her to defer her husband's funeral until his return. He prayed that when he did return he would be bringing with him the two men responsible for murder of his brother and the others.

FIVE

The morning after Al Moody's departure from Lynx Crossing saw the two elder Wilkins brothers leave town and head off down the trail towards Buzzard Gulch. They took with them a good supply of provisions. This was just as well, for, in the event, they were destined to spend two days and two nights camped up on Buzzard Gulch's western ridge. At night, they took it in turn to keep watch, since they were afraid that Luis Bucca might slip through the gulch while they slept. During the day, they passed the time playing checkers, while keeping an eye on the trail. In this manner, Thursday and Friday came and went.

It was while they were breakfasting on coffee, hardtack and beef jerky, early on the Saturday morning, that Jake Wilkins spotted the Mexican.

'Look there,' he hissed, pointing down the trail. 'I reckon that's the sonofabitch at last.'

Seth followed his brother's pointing finger. He gazed at the approaching horseman. A figure, clad all in black from his wide-brimmed sombrero to his shiny leather boots, and riding a coal-black mare, was cantering across the plain towards them. There could be no doubt: this was the long-awaited Luis Bucca.

'We'll wait till the Mexican has ridden right into the gulch,' growled Seth Wilkins. 'Then, when he reaches that bend there, we open fire.' He pointed to a spot in the gulch immediately beneath them.

Jake Wilkins smiled wickedly and nodded his shaggy head.

'It's gonna be dead easy,' he crowed.

'Yup.'

The two brothers picked up their Colt Hartfords and crept forward to the very edge of the gulch's western rim. Crouching down behind a couple of large boulders, they aimed their rifles at the man in black. They kept these trained on him as he rode into the gulch. Once he reached the spot picked out by Seth, they would blast him clean out of the saddle. From that close range such experienced shootists could scarcely miss. Both men grinned.

'We ain't never again gonna earn a thousand dollars as easy as this,' whispered a jubilant Seth Wilkins.

But he was wrong.

Luis Bucca had been a hired gun for a number of

years and he had survived because he took few chances and trusted nobody. One or two of those who had hired him had tried to cheat him out of his blood-money. But not one of them had succeeded. Bucca was determined that, should Al Moody try, he would not succeed either.

The Mexican observed that Buzzard Gulch was just the kind of place where he personally would plan an ambush. Therefore, if Moody were aiming to double-cross him, this would be the natural place along the trail in which to bushwhack him. Consequently, from beneath the wide brim of his sombrero, Bucca carefully scoured both sides of the trail. His keen eyes probed every rock and growth of scrub along the way, then searched up the almost perpendicular sides to where the rims met the clear, azure-blue sky.

Bucca was approximately one hundred yards into the gulch when he spotted it, the unmistakable glint of the sun on a gunbarrel. His instincts had not failed him. Straightaway he leant back in the saddle and pulled the Winchester from his saddle boot. Then, he simply slid from the saddle, dropping to the ground, with the mare between himself and that side of the gulch where he had spotted the revelatory glint. A few quick strides took him into the cover of a scattering of boulders and brush, which lined the edge of the trail. The mare, meantime, trotted a little way and then stopped to graze the sparse tabosa grass.

The Mexican's speedy action took the Wilkins brothers completely by surprise. Neither succeeded in loosing off a shot until after Luis Bucca had vanished into the tumble of boulders. Then, when it was too late, they opened up and a fierce fusillade of shots bounced off the rocks behind which Bucca was crouching.

Bucca grimaced and kept his head down. He waited until the shooting stopped and, once it had, peered from between the boulders at the rocky wall, which reached up to the opposite rim of Buzzard's Gulch. His eyes traversed along the cliff's near-perpendicular length. It looked unscalable until he observed, fifty yards on down the trail, a steeply winding path that led from the gulch floor to the top. A man might surely scramble up that, Bucca thought. He grinned. A plan was forming in his mind.

The Mexican glanced about him. Still keeping his head down, he crawled across to a thicket of mesquite, from which he broke off a thin branch about three feet in length. Taking off his sombrero, he placed this on one end of the stick, which he thereupon proceeded to raise above the level of the boulders in front of him. Then he quickly dropped it again as a couple of bullets rattled into his stone barricade. Again Bucca grinned. The unseen bush-whackers, whoever they were, had taken his bait.

76

Crouching down, Bucca slowly made his way along the gulch in the direction of the winding path. And he was careful to keep a boulder between himself and his would-be assassins each time he quickly raised and dropped the sombrero. This was just as well, for, on each occasion he raised the sombrero, the Wilkins brothers let loose another salvo of shots, all of which either bounced harmlessly off the rocks in front of him or whistled past, to bury themselves in the gulch wall behind Bucca.

Also, immediately after the Colt Hartfords ceased firing, Bucca would respond with his Winchester. Not that he expected to hit anyone. It was rather to let his enemy know that he was still alive. From the frequency of their shots, he guessed that there were two of them. He continued to grin. If his plan succeeded, he would soon learn whether he was correct in this assumption.

In this manner, Bucca proceeded down the trail until eventually he reached a spot exactly opposite the foot of the path. Meantime Seth and Jake Wilkins had expended a large quantity of ammunition as they blasted away with their Colt Hartfords every time Luis Bucca's sombrero popped up into view. But to no avail. None of their many bullets had found its target, so quick had Bucca been each time to withdraw the hat.

Now was the moment in which to put phase two of his plan into action. Bucca once again raised the sombrero above the level of the boulders in front of him. However, this time, he left the hat in full view of his unseen bushwhackers for a fraction longer. This was long enough for Jake Wilkins to draw a bead on it and blast it off the end of the stick. As it flew up into the air, Luis Bucca let out a scream and, on this occasion, he did not respond with his Winchester. Instead, he carefully reloaded the rifle and waited.

Up on the ridge, Seth and Jake Wilkins exchanged glances. Then Seth clapped his brother on the shoulder and exclaimed, 'Goddammit, Jake, I b'lieve you've hit the bastard!'

Jake Wilkins smiled broadly.

'Yeah, I reckon I did,' he replied.

'But we gotta be sure he's good an' dead,' rasped Seth.

'I s'pose.'

'You'd best go an' see.'

'Me?'

'Yup. You can scramble down that there path. I'll keep you covered from up here.'

Jake cautiously peered into the gulch. All was silent below. Surely, Jake reasoned, if the Mexican were still alive, he would have responded by now?

'OK,' he said, although a little reluctantly.

Seth smiled and, standing up in clear view of anyone who might be below, he leant nonchalantly against the nearest boulder and took aim at a spot close to where Luis Bucca's sombrero lay in the dust.

'If the Mexican pops up from behind them there rocks,' he growled, 'I'll shoot his goddam head off.'

'You . . . you figure he will?' Jake enquired, still nervous of exposing himself.

'Nope, I reckon he's dead all right. But we gotta be sure. Also, the boss may ask for proof 'fore he gives us that one thousand dollar pay-out. So, you'd better pick up his sombrero, his handgun an' his boots. That should be proof enough.'

'We could show him the body.'

'Only if we bury it. Otherwise there won't be much left by the time the boss gits back. The buzzards an' the coyotes will see to that.'

'Let's bury it then.'

'We didn't bring no spade with us.'

'No, we didn't.'

'So, git goin', Jake. Like I said, I'll cover you from up here.'

'OK! OK!'

Jake Wilkins rose and laid down the Colt Hartford. The steep path down the side of the gulch was likely to be quite tricky to descend. Consequently, Jake decided he didn't want to be encumbered with the rifle. If Luis Bucca had merely been wounded, he would finish him off from close range with his Remington. Jake slapped the revolver for reassurance and headed towards the spot where the path began.

The bushwhacker's descent was, of necessity, rather slow, for the path was difficult and Jake had no wish to slip and plummet to the foot of the cliff. He proceeded with care and presently reached the floor of the gulch without mishap. Smiling cheerfully, he drew his revolver and walked briskly across the trail towards the sombrero. As he approached it, he observed the bullethole. His smile widened and he skirted the boulder immediately behind the sombrero, expecting to find the dead body of Luis Bucca lying there.

Jake Wilkins discovered, instead, that the Mexican was both alive and well. Indeed, as he rounded the boulder, he found himself staring straight into the barrel of Bucca's Winchester.

'Jeeze!' he exclaimed.

This was the very last word he was to utter. Bucca's first shot hit him in the chest and passed clean through his body, the second took the top of his head off.

From his vantage point at the top of Buzzard Gulch's western rim, Seth Wilkins gazed down in disbelief. Luis Bucca's cunning ploy had completely deceived him. He had been convinced that his brother's shot had killed the Mexican. And, as a result, his response was too late. Before he could squeeze the trigger of his Colt Hartford, Bucca had aimed and fired a third shot. This struck Seth Wilkins in the chest and knocked him flat on his back.

Bucca grinned wickedly and stepped out on to the trail, which he crossed in a few quick strides. Then, he began to clamber up the path towards the summit. Unlike Jake Wilkins, Bucca did not discard his rifle. He was more sure-footed than the heavily built, bearded bushwhacker, and climbed to the rim with comparative ease.

On reaching the top, Bucca cautiously raised his head an inch or two above ground level. He could see Seth Wilkins's feet and the lower part of his legs sticking out from behind a large rock. Bucca eyed them for some moments. There was no sign of any movement. Bucca rose and, holding the Winchester loosely in his right hand, drew the pearl-handled British Tranter with his left. Then, he tiptoed silently across to where Seth Wilkins lay.

That Seth Wilkins was dead there was no doubt. Luis Bucca's third shot had penetrated the bushwhacker's heart. Bucca swore beneath his breath. He had hoped that Seth Wilkins would be mortally wounded but not dead, for he had questions, which he wanted to ask of him.

The similarity between the two dead bushwhackers was unmistakable. Bucca concluded that they were related and, in all probability, brothers. But were they simply road agents who had chosen Buzzard Gulch as the perfect spot in which to ambush unsuspecting travellers? Or were they waiting specifically to waylay and kill him, Luis Bucca?

The Mexican suspected that the latter was the case. And, if it were, then it could only mean one thing: Al Moody had put them up to it.

Luis Bucca dropped the British Tranter back into its holster and reviewed the situation. A confrontation with Al Moody was essential. But common sense decreed that this should take place only after darkness had fallen. To ride into Lynx Crossing during daylight hours would be the height of folly.

Seth Wilkins lay dead on the ridge above Buzzard Gulch while his brother was hidden among the boulders and mesquite that bordered the trail through the gulch. The likelihood of either being discovered by some passing traveller was remote. Luis Bucca smiled coldly and turned and retraced his steps down the path to the trail below.

Once there, he retrieved his sombrero and led his black mare into the cover of the mesquite, where, hidden from view, he waited for darkness to fall.

SIX

Lynx Crossing's Main Street lay in darkness, broken only by a few splashes of yellow light spilling out from the windows and doorways of those premises still open. One such was the Bucking Bronco saloon. Several horses were hitched to the rail outside, for, it being Saturday night, the home-steaders were in town. Luis Bucca hitched his black mare to the rail next to a piebald and clattered up the flight of wooden steps to the stoop.

He crossed the stoop, peered in over the top of the batwing doors and surveyed the scene inside the saloon. The bar-room was nowhere near as crowded as it had been when the herds were still coming. There were, however, a couple of games of poker and blackjack in progress, and there were drinkers at the bar. Joey the bartender had his hands full and, as Bucca watched, he beckoned a bearded, thick-set fellow over. From the look of the fellow, the Mexican guessed that he was related to the two bushwhackers whom he had killed that morning. He was quite right. Joey was talking to their young brother. The bartender was asking Dan Wilkins to fetch a fresh crate of whiskey through to the bar-room.

Upon observing Dan Wilkins vanish through a door next to the bar counter, which obviously led to the saloon's rear quarters, Bucca retreated across the stoop and down the steps to the street. He skirted the horses at the hitching-rail and hurried down the alleyway between the Bucking Bronco and the barbering-parlour next door. Rounding the rear of the saloon, he came upon its back door, which he cautiously pushed open.

Inside was a large storeroom, with another door and a stairway at its far side. To Bucca's left stood several barrels of beer, while to his right were stacked a number of crates of whiskey. Dan Wilkins was in the process of removing one of the latter from the stack when the Mexican walked in through the doorway.

'*Buenas tardes, señor,*' said Bucca, drawing and pointing his revolver at the unsuspecting man.

Wilkins turned abruptly and stared dumb-founded at Bucca, while still holding on to the crate of whiskey. Bucca promptly stepped forward and removed the Remington from Wilkins' holster. Smiling thinly, he tossed the gun into a corner behind the beer barrels.

'You may lower that crate,' he said. 'And then we will have a little talk.' He indicated the stairway. 'Upstairs.'

'Now, look here—' began Wilkins.

'*Señor*, you have a choice,' rasped Bucca. 'You do as I say, or I shoot you.'

Wilkins opened his mouth to protest, but thought better of it. He put down the crate of whiskey and reluctantly began to ascend the stairs. Bucca followed, his British Tranter aimed directly at the centre of Wilkins' back.

At the top of the stairway there was a narrow, ill-lit passage. Doors led off on either side. Bucca indicated that Wilkins should open and enter the first on his left. This proved to be a small bedchamber, containing a narrow bed, one wooden chair and a small dressing-table with a badly cracked mirror.

'Sit down, *señor*,' said Bucca.

Again Wilkins opened his mouth to protest and again he thought better of it He sat down on the wooden chair. Bucca immediately stepped up behind him and, in two swift movements, dropped the revolver back into his holster and pulled the thin bladed knife from the sheath at his waistband. He whipped the knife round in front of Wilkins and drew it across his throat.

'You will answer my questions or I shall slit your throat,' he hissed.

A white-faced Dan Wilkins gulped nervously.

'Wh . . . what d'you wanta know'?' he gasped.

'You have two brothers?' enquired Bucca.

'Y . . . yeah, I have two brothers.'

Bucca laughed harshly.

'You *had* two brothers,' he said. 'Both are dead.'

'Why, you . . . you sonofabitch, I—'

Dan Wilkins's words were cut short as Bucca pulled the blade tight against his throat, drawing blood.

'You will confine yourself to answering my questions,' snarled Bucca. 'Do you understand?'

'Y . . . yes,' croaked Wilkins.

'Your brothers tried to ambush me.'

'Y . . . yes.'

'Why would they do that?'

'The boss asked 'em to.'

'The boss?'

'Al Moody. He owns this here saloon.'

'And you and your brothers were in his pay?'

'Yeah.'

'Why did he want me dead? Did he say?'

'Yeah. He . . . he got a telegram warnin' him you was comin'. He said you was an ol' enemy of his.'

'I see.'

Bucca knew there had been no such telegram. Only he and Al Moody knew he was coming to Lynx Crossing. That had been arranged when Moody and he had met in Wichita to discuss the contract.

Moody had contacted him through a mutual friend and they had agreed to meet in Wichita where neither man was known. Moody had explained that he wanted his brother Lyle killed so that he might inherit the Happy Valley ranch. And, in order that no suspicion should fall on him, he had told Bucca about the regular Wednesday poker-game and had asked Bucca to kill all six players. He had paid the Mexican $1,000 up front, with another $1,000 to come when the job was done.

'Where is Señor Moody'?' enquired Bucca.

'He had another telegram, informin' him that his brother had died. He headed out to attend the funeral, some place down in Texas.'

'Indeed, and how much was he going to pay you to kill me?'

'One thousand bucks.'

Bucca smiled grimly. It had been agreed between them that Al Moody would set off for Texas only after he had paid Bucca his blood-money. The lie about receiving the other wire had evidently been concocted so that the Wilkins brothers would not connect Luis Bucca with the death of Lyle Moody. Since Al Moody had been prepared to pay the brothers $1,000 to kill him, the saloonkeeper had wanted Bucca dead, not to save shelling out the blood-money, but rather to dispose of the only person who could connect him with the massacre in Faro's Creek.

'Thank you, *señor*. You have told me all I need to know,' said Bucaca.

'So . . . so, what happens now?' asked Dan Wilkins fearfully.

'I go south in search of Señor Moody.'

'An' . . . an' I can go?'

'I regret not.'

'But—'

'It is not possible I should let you go.'

'You . . . you said, if'n I didn't answer your questions, you'd slit my throat'

'Yes.'

'Wa'al, I did answer your questions.'

'That is so, *señor*.'

'Therefore, tie me up an' gag me if you think that's necessary. Only don't kill me,' wailed a desperate Dan Wilkins.

Bucca said nothing, but, still smiling grimly, slashed Dan Wilkins's throrat, slitting it from ear to ear. This done, he cleaned the blade on Wilkins's shirt-front and replaced it in its sheath. Then, he dragged the man's corpse off the chair and shoved it beneath the narrow bed. He stood up and made for the door.

It was his intention to leave immediately and ride south to Texas, where he proposed to confront Al Moody on his late brother's Happy Valley ranch. However, as he opened the door, he found his passage blocked by the blonde sporting woman,

Scarlett Duval, and her latest customer, an itinerant cowboy who had stopped off in Lynx Crossing on his way north to find work in Montana.

'What the hell are you doin' in here?' demanded Scarlett.

'I was looking for you, *señorita*,' replied Bucca.

'You could've found me in the bar-room. So, why come sneakin' in by the back door? That's what you did, I reckon,' said the blonde.

'You are correct, *señorita*,' said Bucca. 'I have found that sometimes we Mexicans are not welcome in your gringo saloons. Therefore, being a peaceable kind of a man, I avoid entering them.'

'Then, how come. . . ?'

'I was walking past and, upon glancing inside, I saw you, *señorita*. I guessed that, sooner or later, your profession would take you upstairs.'

'An' you jest sneaked in the back an' headed up here to wait for me?'

'Yes.'

'Wa'al, she's with me,' said the cowboy belligerently.

'Are you a gambling man?' enquired Bucca.

The cowboy shot him a long, hard look.

'What if I am?' he growled.

'I suggest we toss a coin to see who enjoys the lady's favours first.'

Bucca produced a silver dollar.

'I dunno?'

'Win or lose, after the toss, the coin is yours, *señor*,' stated the Mexican.

The cowboy relented. He badly wanted to get into bed with the blonde, yet, for the price of a dollar, he was prepared, if necessary, to postpone that pleasure for half an hour or so.

'OK,' he said. 'It's a deal.'

Bucca smiled.

'Your call,' he said.

'Heads!' cried the cowboy.

Bucca tossed the coin, deftly caught it and slapped it on to the back of his band.

'Tails,' said Bucca quietly.

The cowboy scowled.

'So, if you will excuse us?' Luis Bucca handed him the silver dollar and glanced meaningfully towards the door.

'I'll see you later,' said the cowboy to Scarlett, then he turned on his heel and left.

'And now, *señorita*. . . .' began Bucca, as he advanced upon the blonde.

Scarlett held out her hand.

'Pay first, pleasure later,' she said firmly.

Bucca smiled and shrugged his shoulders.

'How much?' he asked.

'Five dollars.'

Bucca guessed that this was rather more than she usually asked. But he did not demur. He handed the woman the money, which she promptly stuck in the top drawer of her dressing-table. Then, smiling seductively at him, Scarlett began slowly to undress.

Since Scarlett Duval was a sporting woman who actually enjoyed her work, she invariably performed well. Her intercourse with Luis Bucca was no exception and when, twenty minutes later, the session ended, the Mexican's carnal desires had certainly been fully satisfied. He rose from the bed, feeling both relaxed and replete.

The woman remained in bed while Luis Bucca dressed. Then, when he was about to leave, she smiled up at him and murmured, 'You are quite a man, Mr Mexican!'

Bucca smiled back.

'And you are quite a woman!' he responded.

Thereupon he turned and left the room.

Fate plays many strange tricks. It did that night in Lynx Crossing. As Luis Bucca was making his way back along the alley towards Main Street, Will Devine and Jack Stone were entering through the batwing doors of the Bucking Bronco saloon. They had ridden hard and fast from Faro's Creek in the hope of finding Luis Bucca and Al Moody closeted together. And they had hitched their exhausted horses to the same rail as that to which Bucca had earlier tied his black mare.

They missed each other by a mere matter of seconds. Bucca mounted the mare and cantered out of Lynx Crossing, blissfully unaware of his pursuers. Will Devine and Jack Stone, in the meantime, crossed the bar-room and accosted Joey the bartender.

'I believe Al Moody owns this here saloon,' said Stone.

'That's right. You friends of his?' enquired Joey.

'Not exactly,' replied Stone.

'But we're lookin' for him,' said Devine.

The bartender eyed the two strangers curiously and with a feeling of some apprehension. He figured they could be trouble, and he wished fervently that Marshal Matt Cozens would put in an appearance. However, there being no sign of the peace-officer, Joey decided to be as co-operative as possible.

'Mr Moody ain't in town,' he informed them.

'No?' said Stone.

'Nope. He left a few days back. Seems he got a wire tellin' him that his brother had died. He set off to arrange an' attend the funeral. Some place down in Texas.'

'Goddammit, we must've missed him on the trail!' exclaimed Devine.

'Yeah, wa'al, there's more'n jest the one trail. He obviously took a different trail from the one we were followin', otherwise we'd have met him head on,' commented Stone.

'Hell!'

'Say we take off back the way we came an' Moody

returns north after the funeral, we could miss each other again.'

'So, whaddya suggest, Jack?'

'We could wait here till he gits back.'

'What about Bucca? We'd hoped to catch the two of 'em together.'

'That's true.' The Kentuckian turned to the bartender. 'Did a Mexican dressed all in black ride into town jest prior to Mr Moody's departure?' he asked.

'Not to my knowledge,' declared Joey. 'Did this Mexican an' Mr Moody have some kinda business together?'

'I guess you could say that,' rasped Stone.

'Wa'al, I s'pose they could've met in secret. After dark mebbe? Or outa town?'

'Is there anyone likely to know if they did?'

'Yeah. An associate of Moody's, say,' suggested Devine.

'Wa'al, Mr Moody did leave the Wilkins brothers in charge of the saloon.'

'The Wilkins brothers. An' jest where might they be'?' enquired Stone, glancing round the bar-room.

'Seth an' Jake, they took off on the mornin' after Mr Moody left. An' as far as I know, they ain't been back since,' said Joey.

'So, who's in charge now? You?' growled Devine.

The bartender shook his head.

'Nope. Dan, the youngest brother, he's in charge.'

'Then, where is he?' demanded Stone.

'That's a good question. I asked him to fetch me a crate of whiskey a while back. He's sure takin' his time.'

'Where do you keep your whiskey?'

'Through that there door.' Joey indicated the door next to the bar with a jerk of his thumb. 'There's a storeroom at the back of the saloon.'

'Thanks.' Stone smiled at the bartender and asked quietly, 'Is it OK if'n we go through?'

Joey reckoned they would go through with or without his say-so. So, he smiled back and replied, 'Sure thing, gents. An' when you see Dan, tell him to hurry up with that there whiskey. I'm down to the last bottle.'

'Will do,' said Stone.

With Will Devine close on his heels, the Kentuckian pushed open the door and plunged into the Bucking Bronco's rear quarters. There was a short passage, at the end of which stood another door. The two men went through this and found themselves in the storeroom. They observed the beer barrels and the stack of whiskey crates, noting that one crate had been removed and stood on its own in the centre of the room.

Jack Stone called out.

'Dan Wilkins!'

There was no reply, so the Kentuckian repeated the call.

'Dan Wilkins!'

Again there was no response.

'Shall we try up there?' Will Devine pointed at the stairway. 'Whaddya think?'

'Yeah, let's do that.'

Both men felt instinctively that something was amiss, though neither could have said just why they had that feeling. They drew their revolvers and, with Stone leading, slowly made their way upstairs.

At the head of the stairs the pair paused and peered down the dimly lit passage. As they hesitated regarding which door they should push open, the door to the first bedchamber on their left suddenly swung back and Scarlett Duval stood before them.

The blonde had dressed and repaired her make-up following her session with Luis Bucca. Now she was ready to go down and inform the cowboy that his turn was due. A look of surprise spread across her pretty face upon her being so unexpectedly confronted by Will Devine and the tough-looking Kentuckian.

'Sorry to startle you, ma'am,' said Devine, politely removing his hat.

'W . . . what are you doin' up here?' gasped the blonde.

'We're lookin' for someone.'

'An' jest who might you be lookin' for?'

'A feller by the name of Dan Wilkins.'

Scarlett smiled.

'I don't think you'll find him up here,' she said.

'No?'

'No.' She threw the bedroom door wide open and said, by way of a jest, 'You can look under my bed, why don't you?'

The two men grinned. Then, Will Devine, entering into the spirit of the joke, replied, 'Why not?' and did just that.

'Holy cow!' he yelled, straightening up and staring wide-eyed at the blonde.

'What's the matter?' she cried.

'Is . . . is Dan Wilkins a thick-set young feller with a black bushy beard?' he enquired.

'Yeah, that 'bout describes Dan,' said Scarlett.

'Then, that's precisely where he is.'

'Under my bed?' exclaimed the blonde.

'Yup. An' with his throat slit from ear to ear,' said Devine.

'Oh, my God! We . . . we'd best call the marshal.'

'Reckon we had. What d'you say, Jack?'

The Kentuckian nodded.

'I'm only guessin',' he said, 'but I think Luis Bucca's been here before us. An' only jest before us.'

'You think that he. . . ?'

'Yeah, Will, I figure he slit that feller's throat.'

'Who . . . who is this Luis Bucca?' asked Scarlett.

'A Mexican shootist who done a deal with Al

96

Moody. My guess is the Mexican was expectin' Moody to pay for services rendered, but Moody decided to double-cross him.'

'With the help of the Wilkins brothers!' cried Devine.

'Exactly. Two of 'em left town a few days back an' ain't been seen since. If they set out to ambush Bucca, they sure picked the wrong man.'

'You figure they're dead?' gasped Scarlett.

'Gotta be,' said Stone.

'An' this . . . this Luis Bucca?'

'He'll be on his way south, hopin' to catch up with Al Moody.'

'We could only have missed the murderin' varmint by a few minutes!' declared Devine.

'You did,' said Scarlett. 'He was with me just now. In that there bed.'

'So, let's git goin'. He ain't that far ahead of us,' said Devine.

'We only jest got here. Our hosses are plumb exhausted. They wouldn't last above a coupla miles. Let's call the marshal an' explain things to him, then grab ourselves some supper. After that, with the hosses rested, we'll set out.'

Devine reflected on the Kentuckian's proposition.

'OK,' he said at last. 'Guess you're right, Jack. We cain't afford to ride our hosses into the ground. It's one helluva long ways back to Texas.'

Consequently, by the time the pair eventually hit the trail south, Luis Bucca, the Devil's Left Hand, had several hours' start on them.

SEVEN

It was mid-morning three days later when Luis Bucca found himself approaching the outskirts of Faro's Creek. He had had a long, hard, dusty ride and was keen to confront his double-crosser. But he dared not ride into town, for he was sure to be recognized and would be most unlikely to get out alive.

As he considered what to do, he spotted a lone figure driving a buckboard and fast approaching along a converging trail. This was George Blake, a local homesteader, who, dressed in his Sunday best, was on his way into town to attend the funeral of his neighbour, Lyle Moody.

Bucca urged his mare forward and blocked the other's path where the two trails met. George Blake reined in his horses and gazed in some alarm at the black-clad stranger. He had not been in Faro's Creek on the day of the massacre at the Longhorn saloon, but the man before him matched exactly the description he had been given of the killer.

'*Buenos dias, señor,*' said Bucca.

'Er . . . good . . . good day, stranger,' stammered a nervous George Blake.

'You are heading into town?'

'Yes . . . yes, I am aimin' to attend my neighbour's funeral.'

'And who might your neighbour be?'

'Lyle Moody. He owns . . . er . . . owned the Happy Valley ranch, right next to my place.'

'Indeed? And does that trail you have just passed along lead to the Happy Valley ranch?'

'Yeah, it sure does.'

'Thank you. That is all I wished to know.'

'Wa'al, if you'd kindly stand aside so as I can proceed, I'd be obliged.'

'I do not think so *señor*.'

'But . . . but why not? I . . . I—'

'You know who I am.'

'No, no, I ain't got no idea who you are!' protested the homesteader, who, by now, was absolutely certain that the Mexican was none other than the assassin known as the Devil's Left Hand.

'You lie, *señor*.'

As he shouted this denial, George Blake attempted to surreptitiously grab hold of the shot-gun, which lay behind him in the buckboard. But he was too late. Bucca had already drawn his pearl handled British Tranter. The Mexican fired twice in quick succession. The first shot hit Blake in the chest, while the second drilled a hole in the centre of his forehead and blasted his brains out of the back of his skull.

Before Blake's horses could bolt, Bucca rode forward and grabbed hold of their reins. Then he leapt from the mare on to the buckboard. He seated himself and drove the buckboard towards a small stand of cottonwood trees, some fifty yards or so away to the south side of the trail. Having hidden the cart in the midst of these trees, Bucca returned to the trail and remounted his mare.

As he did so, the Mexican observed a small group of riders proceeding along the trail from the same direction as that taken by George Blake. He immediately turned the mare's head and trotted off into the stand of cottonwood. There, hidden from sight, Bucca was able to watch the riders as they passed on their way to Faro's Creek. There were nine altogether. Eight he assumed to be employees, cowhands and the like, from the Happy Valley ranch. The ninth he recognized as Al Moody.

Bucca waited until the nine had crossed the town limits and vanished into Faro's Creek. Then he emerged from the trees and took the trail towards the Happy Valley ranch.

It was a ride of approximately four miles, passing *en route* the homestead of the late George Blake.

The ranch's name was apt, for it lay in a pleasant, grassy valley with a stream meandering through. There was a ranch house, a bunkhouse, a cook-house, several barns and outbuildings, stables and a large corral. A number of fine-looking mustangs were contained in the corral, while several hundred head of prime cattle happily grazed within the confines of the valley.

Bucca smiled. So, this was Al Moody's inheritance! He urged the mare forward and rode up to the ranch house. As he had suspected, the ranch was deserted. Al Moody and everyone else on the ranch were evidently attending Lyle Moody's funeral.

He rode round to the rear of the ranch house, dismounted and hobbled the mare there, where she could not be seen by Al Moody and the others upon their return from the funeral. Bucca wanted his presence to remain a secret from everyone except Al Moody. And he also intended that it should come as a surprise, not to say a shock, to the new owner of the Happy Valley ranch.

The Mexican strolled slowly round to the front of the ranch house and climbed up the steps onto the stoop. He tried the door. It was unlocked. He stepped inside. Considering that Al Moody's brother had remained a bachelor, the ranch house was remarkably well-furnished and comfortable. Bucca helped himself to a glass of brandy from the rancher's sideboard and then lowered himself into a large brown-leather armchair to await Al Moody's return.

It was shortly after noon when Moody and the others rode back onto the ranch. The thunder of their horses' hooves alerted Luis Bucca and he rose and went across to the window. The nine drew up in front of the ranch house, whereupon Moody conversed for a minute or two with a tall, lean cowboy, whom Bucca guessed to be the ranch foreman.

Once the conversation ceased, the tall, lean cowboy and his fellows rode off towards the bunkhouse, while Al Moody dismounted and, having hitched his horse to the rail outside, headed up the steps and into the ranch house.

'*Buenos dias*, Señor Moody,' said Bucca.

Al Moody gasped and his right hand automatically dropped to his thigh. He had forgotten momentarily that he was not carrying a gun. He had not expected to have need of one at his brother's funeral. It had been an instinctive move and one which he realized made no sense, for he could never have hoped to out-draw the Mexican.

'Er . . . good . . . good day, Luis. What . . . what a pleasant surprise,' said Moody, forcing a smile.

'It was part of our deal that you should await my arrival in Lynx Crossing,' said Bucca.

'Yes . . . er . . . yes, so it was.'

'And that you should pay me the one thousand dollars, which you owed me.'

'Er . . . yes, I guess so.'

'Instead, you planned to have me killed.'

'No. I swear—'

'Do not lie.'

'But—'

'I know that you had two men, brothers, lie in wait for me in a gulch just outside of the town. They were to kill me. But, in fact, I killed them.'

'Jeeze!'

'You do not deny it?'

' 'Course I deny it. They were probably jest a coupla road agents, an' merely picked on you by chance.'

'And the third brother?'

'The third brother! Whaddya mean?'

'He remained in town.'

'So?'

'He told me everything.'

'I . . . I see. Wa'al. Luis, it ain't quite what it seems. Y'see—'

'No lies, if you please, Señor Moody.'

'Luis, I—'

'I said, no lies.' Bucca glared at his erstwhile employer. 'I know why you wanted me dead,' he added.

'You . . . you do?'

'Yes. I am the only person who can link you to the

killings in the Longhorn saloon.'

'I guess you are.'

'You know I am. And, with me dead, you were confident that nobody could prove your guilt. There were those who might suspect that you had hired me to kill your brother and the others, yet they would need proof if they wished to convict you.'

'Yeah, they would.'

'I could give them that proof.'

'Not without incriminatin' yourself, Luis.'

'Oh, but it is already known that I am the assassin!' Bucca laughed harshly. 'An affidavit from me would hang you.'

'It would be real risky handin' in such a document. You could be caught, arrested an' hanged yourself,' said Moody.

Again Bucca laughed.

'Perhaps, yet it would be a risk worth the taking. You double-crossed me, Señor Moody. Instead of paying me what you owed, you tried to have me killed.'

'So . . . so, what are you gonna do?'

'I should kill you.'

'Look . . . look, I'll pay you the one thousand dollars.' A note of desperation had crept into Al Moody's voice. ' 'Deed, I'll do better'n that. I'll pay you two thousand!' he cried.

The Mexican shook his head.

'No,' he said. 'That is not enough.'

'Three thou—'

'Silence!' Bucca grinned as his terrified betrayer clamped shut his mouth. 'Now, I will tell you what you will do if you wish to live,' he hissed. 'I assume that you do not intend to take over your brother's mantle and actively run this ranch?'

Al Moody, white-faced and trembling, shook his head.

'You propose to sell the ranch, yes?'

'Yeah.'

'Good! It will fetch many dollars.'

'I s'pose.'

'Whatever you get, you will split fifty-fifty with me.'

Al Moody's jaw dropped.

'I . . . I dunno. Mebbe seventy-thirty?'

'You are in no position to bargain, Señor Moody. It will be fifty-fifty, or I kill you.'

Al Moody gulped. The look in Luis Bucca's pitiless coal-black eyes told Moody that, should he refuse, he was a dead man.

'OK,' he croaked. 'It . . . it's a deal.'

'And this time there will be no double-cross.'

'No, I swear it!'

'There will be no double-cross because you will sell the ranch to my uncle.'

'Your uncle! An' jest who in blue blazes is your uncle that he can afford the price I'll want for the Happy Valley?'

'Don Pedro Gomez. You have heard of him?'

Al Moody nodded.

'Yeah,' he said. 'I've heard of him.'

He recalled, from the time when he was still living in Texas, that Don Pedro Gomez was reputed to be the wealthiest rancher south of the Rio Grande, and wealthier than any in all Texas. He had an enormous spread of several thousand acres in the Coahuila province of Mexico.

'It is agreed, then?' said Bucca.

'But jest why would your uncle wanta buy the Happy Valley? Hell, he's so goddam rich already, he don't need to go buyin' up no Texas spread!'

'It is not a question of need.'

'No?'

'No. It would be a feather in his cap to acquire land in the United States. One in the eye for the gringos, eh?' Bucca laughed 'So, Señor Moody, what do you say?' he asked.

Al Moody realized he had no choice. And he had to concede that fifty per cent of whatever Don Pedro Gomez was willing to pay would still be a fortune.

'You promise that, after you have your money, you will not kill me?' he said.

'You have the word of Luis Bucca.'

With this Moody had to be content. He had broken his word. How could he be sure that Bucca wouldn't break his? He could not be sure; he could only hope. With the money in his pocket, the Mexican could easily decide either to betray Moody to the forces of law and order or simply to kill him.

'How do I contact your uncle?' enquired Moody.

'I shall take you to him.'

'When?'

'Now.'

Bucca grabbed Al Moody by the arm and led him across the room to the rear window. Moody observed the hobbled mare.

'Your hoss?'

'Yes, Señor Moody. I shall ride her up on to those bluffs yonder.' He pointed to the cliffs overlooking the south side of the valley. 'You will advise your men that you are proposing to sell the ranch to my uncle and are setting off immediately for Mexico to arrange the sale. Then, you will join me on the bluffs and we will ride together to the Rancho Conchos. Agreed?'

Al Moody nodded reluctantly.

'Agreed,' he said.

'I shall go, then,' said Bucca. 'But beware, my friend, of attempting a second double-cross. Should you do so, I will certainly kill you.'

He stared hard at Moody before releasing his arm and slipping swiftly out of the ranch house's rear door. Moments later, the black mare was freed from her hobbling and the Mexican was climbing into the saddle. He dug his heels into the mare's ribs and they set off at a gallop towards the distant bluffs.

Al Moody watched them go. He was still trembling. He went across and helped himself to a stiff measure of the brandy, which Bucca had earlier been sampling. It took a second measure before Moody had ceased to tremble and the colour had returned to his cheeks. Hoping that he looked more like his old self, he left the ranch house and went in search of his foreman.

He found him in one of the barns, supervising the repair of a wagon wheel.

Bill Lawton had been Lyle Moody's foreman for the best part of a decade. Tall and lean, with keen blue eyes and a rugged, weather-beaten visage, Lawton was dressed in the usual cowboy attire of Stetson, check shirt, denim pants and chaps. He looked up as Al Moody entered the barn.

'Howdy, Mr Moody, what can I do for you?' he enquired.

'Wa'al, it's like this, Bill,' explained Moody. 'I ain't cut out to be a rancher like my brother was.'

'No?'

'Nope. Jest ain't my style. So, I figure I'd best sell the ranch.'

'An' jest where does that leave me an' the boys?' demanded Lawton.

'Exactly where you are, I guess. The feller I have in mind to buy it is Don Pedro Gomez.'

The foreman whistled softly.

'Wow! You sure he's a likely buyer?'

'Pretty darned sure. An', if he does buy the ranch, wa'al, I reckon he'll want you an' the boys to carry on runnin' it, jest like now. 'Course, he'll wanta stick his oar in from time to time, 'bout buyin' in new stock an' sellin' the beef up north, that kinda thing.'

'I guess.'

'But, for the most part, I figure you'll be given a pretty free rein.'

'You think so?'

'I do.'

'OK, I wish you luck then.'

'Thanks, Bill. I figure there ain't no point in delayin' matters, so I'm gonna set out for Don Pedro's hacienda right away. I'll leave you in charge of the ranch till I git back.'

'You can rely on me, Mr Moody.'

'I'm sure I can.'

With these words, Al Moody retraced his steps to the ranch house and unhitched his horse from the rail outside. He mounted and set off towards the bluffs, which Luis Bucca had pointed out to him.

The two men met as arranged, the one eager to be on his way, the other rather less so. Moody still had misgivings, but he had committed himself and, consequently, there was no going back.

'How many days' ride to your uncle's ranch, Luis?' he asked.

'Four, five days,' said Bucca.

'Then, let's git goin'.'

'*Pronto, señor.*'

They rode down on to the plains and took the trail south towards Mexico.

EIGHT

Don Pedro Gomez sat on the veranda of his white-washed villa, in the heart of his extensive hacienda. He was enjoying the late morning sunshine and watching his eldest son, Roberto, breaking in a wild mustang. The beast was a black stallion, full of fire and spirit, and not easily subdued.

Don Pedro smiled happily. He had, over the years, built up the largest herd of cattle in Coahuila province and his future was secured. Also, he enjoyed a happy marriage, his wife Maria was both loving and kind, and he had three fine sons and two daughters who, taking after their mother, were very beautiful.

He himself was a man of no more than average height, yet he possessed a certain charisma and authority that marked him out as a figure of influence and power. His darkly handsome and urbane countenance was clean-shaven, his thick head of hair snowy-white and immaculately cut, and he was attired in the finest apparel: a low-crowned black sombrero, a black jacket, vest and trousers of the best cloth and soft-leather shiny black boots. Don Pedro did not carry a gun. He had no need.

His son, Roberto, was no less splendidly attired, although his clothes were his working attire, and so a little worn. Roberto was black-haired and a few inches taller than his father, yet possessing a similar slender frame. His litheness, combined with an unusual strength, made him into a formidable horseman. And this he needed to be, to break in a horse of the black stallion's mettle.

The breaking-in of the mustang took some considerable time and Don Pedro was on to his second cigar when, just as Roberto sensed he had almost tamed the stallion, a small cavalcade of horsemen appeared in the distance. As they approached, Don Pedro recognized his nephew, Luis Bucca, who was riding with a gringo and escorted by his two younger sons and half a dozen *vaqueros*.

The cavalcade thundered to a halt and, leaping from the saddle, Luis Bucca saluted the rancher.

'*Buenos dias*, Uncle!' he cried.

Don Pedro's brow darkened. He glared at the younger man. He had hoped never again to see this miscreant who had brought shame and dishonour on the family and an early death to his heartbroken mother, Don Pedro's sainted sister.

'What do you want, Luis?' he rasped.

Bucca smiled.

'Come now, Uncle, what kind of a greeting is that? It is as well that my friend does not speak Spanish. Otherwise, he might think that we are not welcome.'

Don Pedro transferred his gaze to Al Moody. He did not like what he saw. The man had shifty eyes and a mean look about him. Another as ruthless and destitute of virtue as his nephew, Don Pedro decided. Nevertheless, honour demanded that he show courtesy to the stranger at his door.

'I understand, *señor*, that you speak no Spanish,' he said in perfect English to Al Moody. 'Therefore, we shall speak in English.'

'Thank you, Don Pedro,' said Moody and dismounting, he climbed up on to the veranda and shook the rancher by the hand.

Don Pedro gestured that Roberto should join them and, when he had handed over the stallion to one of the *vaqueros*, the young man left the corral and headed towards the ranch house. His two younger brothers also dismounted and clambered up on to the veranda while the remaining *vaqueros* turned around and galloped off in a cloud of dust. They had spotted Luis Bucca and Al Moody riding on to Don Pedro's land and, at the command of his sons, had surrounded the pair and escorted them to the ranch house. Now they were free to return to their normal duties.

Luis Bucca, undeterred by his cool reception, proceeded to introduce Al Moody to his four relatives, Don Pedro, Roberto and the two younger brothers, Ricardo and Raimundo.

When these formalities had been completed, Don Pedro offered his visitors a drink. Although neither Bucca nor Moody observed him issue any order, nonetheless the drinks appeared only moments later; long, slim glasses of lemonade brought by one of his maidservants. Moody had expected beer or perhaps whiskey. However, he had to concede that the cool, refreshing lemonade was the perfect drink to soothe his parched throat.

'So, Luis,' said Don Pedro, 'to what do we owe the pleasure of your visit?'

If Bucca observed the note of sarcasm in his uncle's voice, he chose to ignore it. 'Señor Moody has recently inherited a ranch. He wishes to sell it. I suggested that you might buy this ranch, Uncle.'

Don Pedro's eyes narrowed.

'And why would I want to do that? I already own the largest ranch in Coahuila,' he murmured.

'It would be one on the eye for the gringos.'

'Yes.'

'Also, the cattle there could be sold up north. This would provide you with another, very lucrative market. You would earn many, many American dollars from the sale of the Texas longhorns.'

'Yes.'

'So, what do you say, Uncle?'

'I do not need American dollars.'

'No, of course not, yet. . . .'

'What is your concern in all of this, Luis?'

'Señor Moody is proposing to pay me a proportion of the sale price.'

'And why should you do that, Señor Moody?' enquired Don Pedro, eyeing the erstwhile saloon-keeper suspiciously.

'Wa'al, your . . . er . . . your nephew, he did me a certain service for which I'm mighty grateful.'

'Indeed?'

'Yeah. An' so, when I sell the ranch, I'll be in a position to pay him what I owe.'

'And how much would that be?'

'There is no exact figure, Uncle,' said Bucca.

'No?'

'No.'

'So, do you have a particular proportion of the sale price in mind?'

'Yes, Uncle. Fifty per cent.'

Don Pedro scowled, while his three sons stared in amazement at their cousin.

'Fifty per cent?' said the rancher, glancing from his nephew to Al Moody.

'That . . . that's right, Don Pedro,' affirmed Moody nervously.

'This ranch, it is how big?'

'I ain't exactly sure. It ain't as big as your spread, but I figure it covers a few thousand acres an' there's several hundred head of cattle. Also, the Happy Valley has some of the best grazin' land in all Texas. 'Deed, it's aptly named.'

'Then, it will command a very good price.'

'Yeah.'

'My nephew must have done you a considerable service for you to pay him one half of whatever you may get for the Happy Valley ranch.'

'Er . . . yeah, he did.'

Don Pedro eyed Luis Bucca, his face expressing his distaste.

'I do not think that I want to know the nature of this service,' he said quietly.

'No?'

'No.'

'So, what do you say, Uncle, about buying the ranch off Señor Moody?' enquired Bucca eagerly.

Don Pedro closed his eyes and considered the matter for some moments. He had no real wish to have any dealings with the American, whom he regarded as someone without honour, yet he felt that he must do just that. He opened his eyes and stared hard at Luis Bucca.

'You have brought shame to my family, Luis,' he said. 'My only consolation is that you do not share my good name. Nevertheless, you are related, a fact

117

which I deplore.'

'Oh, come now, Uncle. . . !'

'Silence! Your life of crime broke your mother's heart and brought about her premature death. Do you deny that?'

Luis Bucca decided that to protest would be futile.

'No, Uncle,' he replied.

'Should I purchase Señor Moody's ranch and you receive half of what I pay him, this will make you a wealthy man.'

'Yes, Uncle,' said Bucca.

'It will give you sufficient to live the rest of your life in comfort.'

'That is true.'

'You will, consequently, have no need to continue with your life of crime.'

'No.'

'Do I have your word, Luis, that, in these circumstances, you will abandon for ever this damnable way of life?'

Bucca smiled inwardly. Outwardly, he remained quite impassive.

'You have my word, Uncle,' he declared.

Don Pedro, who was nobody's fool, placed no trust in his nephew's word, but hoped that, as a rich man, Luis Bucca would be too busy enjoying life to break his promise.

'Very well,' he said, 'I shall consider making this

purchase. But I do this only in memory of your sainted mother, my sister, may she rest in peace. Were it not for her, I should not raise a finger to help you.'

'No, Uncle.'

'And I shall not buy if the ranch and the deal are not to my liking. You will get a fair price, Señor Moody, but no more than that.'

Al Moody nodded.

'That's OK by me,' he said. 'A fair price is all I ask for.'

He was mightily relieved. The Wilkins brothers' failure to murder Luis Bucca had put his life in jeopardy. Indeed, he feared that Bucca still harboured a desire to kill him. However, until Bucca received his share of the purchase money, the Mexican was obliged to hold fire. When the money was paid over, Moody would ask Don Pedro for an escort of *vaqueros* to take him safely back across the border. And, once in the United States, he would head straightway for one of the East Coast cities, probably either New York or Boston, where Bucca would be most unlikely to find him.

It was at this point that Roberto intervened.

'Suppose you do buy the Happy Valley ranch, Father,' he said. 'Who will run it? I have no desire to live in Texas and I do not think that my brothers have either.'

'No, I certainly do not,' agreed Ricardo.

'Nor I,' added Raimundo.

'That's OK, Don Pedro. I have left the ranch in the care of Bill Lawton, who has been foreman there for many years. He and his men can easily cope with the day-to-day runnin' of the ranch. An occasional visit from you or one of your sons will surely be all that's needed,' said Moody.

'This Bill Lawton, he is trustworthy?' demanded Don Pedro Gomez.

'Yeah, he sure is,' replied Moody, who would have sworn that a rattlesnake was harmless, had he needed to do so to close the deal.

'Hmm. How long is it since you inherited the ranch?' enquired Don Pedro.

'Oh . . . er . . . a li'l while.'

'How little a while?'

'Wa'al, I s'pose a week or two now.'

Don Pedro smiled. It was evident that the American's word was about as worthless as his nephew's.

'Roberto,' he said, 'you are a good judge of men.'

'Yes, Father.'

'I want you to ride to this Happy Valley ranch. Señor Moody will give you directions how to find it.'

'Of course, Don Pedro,' said Moody.

'And, once there, I want you to assess it, Roberto, and consider whether it is worth purchasing.'

'Yes, Father.'

'If it is, then you will calculate a fair price. And,

120

while you are there, you will closely observe Señor Lawton and determine whether or not I may safely leave him and his men in charge of the ranch. Is that understood?'

'It is. When do I leave?'

'I suggest tomorrow at first light.'

'Very well.'

'You will need a note from Señor Moody to hand to his foreman, informing him of the purpose of your visit.'

'I could mebbe ride with him an'—' began Moody.

'No, you will remain here as my guest until Roberto returns.'

'Wa'al, I dunno. It—'

'It will save you a long, dusty ride there and back.'

'I s'pose.'

'Since my sons and I have a ranch to run, we shall have to leave you very much to your own devices for the duration of your stay.' Don Pedro smiled and added drily, 'However, you will at least have your dear friend, my nephew Luis, for a companion.'

Luis Bucca grinned. He had by no means forgiven Moody and intended to make his stay as unpleasant as possible.

'That will be nice, won't it, Señor Moody?' he hissed.

Al Moody forced a wry smile.

'Yes, Luis,' he replied unhappily.

And so it was settled. The matter of the sale would remain in abeyance until Roberto Gomez returned from his mission across the border.

NINE

Will Devine and Jack Stone rode on to the Happy Valley spread and up to the ranch house, where they were met by Bill Lawton. He immediately recognized Devine.

'Howdy, Mr Devine,' he said. 'It was a bad business 'bout your brother an' the others. I don't s'pose you've heard whether the law's caught up with that murderin' Mexican?'

'No, Bill, I ain't,' said Devine.

'Hmm. I still ain't got over Mr Moody's death. He was a darned good boss.'

'Yeah. Wa'al, I guess it's his brother Al who's your boss now. He's gotta be the new owner of the Happy Valley.'

'Not for long.'

'No?'

'Nope. He took off a few hours back to arrange its sale. 'Deed, we hadn't been back more'n an hour

from his brother's funeral when he informed me he
was sellin' up.'

'That was kinda sudden, surely?'

'Yeah. It seemed so, though mebbe he'd been
mullin' the matter over in his head 'fore then. I
dunno.'

'So, he's got a buyer?'

'Sure has. Don Pedro Gomez.'

'Holy cow! Don Pedro owns most of Coahuila
province. His spread is goddam enormous!'

'Yup.'

'An' Al Moody took off there an' then for Mexico?'

'That's what I said.'

'An' he was on his own?'

'Yeah. Who would he be with?'

Will Devine glanced knowingly at Jack Stone.

'We think there's mebbe a go-between,'
explained the Kentuckian. 'Shall we tell him?' he
enquired of Devine.

Devine nodded.

'You asked about Luis Bucca,' he said. 'Wa'al, me
an' Jack trailed him all the ways up to Lynx
Crossing, a one-time cow town in Kansas.'

'What in tarnation was he doin' there?'
exclaimed Lawton.

'We reckon he was aimin' to collect his blood-
money.'

'Whaddya mean?'

'He's a professional assassin. He was paid to shoot

my brother, your boss, an' the rest of them poker-players in the Longhorn saloon.'

'But why?'

'D'you know where Al Moody has been livin' these past few years?'

'Nope. He didn't say.'

'Wa'al, it was Lynx Crossing.'

You mean that he. . . ?'

'Yeah. Al Moody hired Luis Bucca.'

'It's our guess,' interjected Stone, 'that he figured, if'n the Mexican killed all six poker-players, nobody would be able to prove who exactly was behind the killin's.'

'This was all so as he'd inherit the Happy Valley spread from his brother?'

'You got it, Bill,' said Devine.

'Unfortunately, we missed Bucca, though we know he visited Lynx Crossing. So, we trailed him back south,' said Stone.

'Could he have met up with Al Moody?' asked Devine.

Bill Lawton pondered this question.

'I . . . I s'pose he could,' he said eventually. 'If he'd hidden hisself somewheres on the ranch while we was attendin' Lyle Moody's funeral.'

'That would explain Al Moody's sudden decision to head south for Mexico. Mebbe there's some connection between him an' Don Pedro Gomez?' said Devine.

'Other than them both bein' Mexican?' murmured Stone. 'Yeah, my guess is Bucca and Moody rode south together.'

'Goddammit!' cried Devine. 'We missed Bucca by a matter of minutes in Lynx Crossing an' now we've missed him again, this time by only a few hours! If only we hadn't delayed leavin' Lynx Crossing!'

'Our bosses were plumb exhausted. We could've pursued Bucca straight away, but, if'n we hadn't caught up with him almost at once, they'd have given out on us. In which case, we wouldn't be here yet,' said the Kentuckian.

'No, you're right, Jack,' conceded Devine. 'We had to rest up. But what do we do now, head for Mexico an' Don Pedro's hacienda?'

Stone shook his head.

'No,' he said, 'for we don't know what kinda reception we'd git.'

'I b'lieve Don Pedro is an honest, law-abidin' kinda feller,' declared Devine.

'Mebbe so. But still, I figure we let him come to us, Will.'

'Whaddya mean?'

'He ain't gonna buy no pig in a poke. He's gonna wanta see what he's gittin'.'

'I guess.'

'So, he an' Al Moody will, like as not, be here in a few days' time.'

'An' Bucca?'

126

'He won't be far away.'

'Wa'al, Mr Devine, you an' your friend are welcome to stay here on the ranch until they come,' said Lawton.

'Yeah, an' since that's gonna be some while off, you'll have time to arrange John's funeral 'fore then,' stated Stone.

Will Devine nodded.

'Yeah,' he said. 'I need to do that.'

He and Stone accepted Bill Lawton's offer, Stone was properly introduced to the foreman and, with their accommodation settled, the pair headed for Faro's Creek in order to visit the mortician, Barnaby Jones.

The necessary arrangements were then made and, a couple of days later, at about the same time that Luis Bucca and Al Moody reached the perimeter of Don Pedro Gomez's vast spread, the funeral of John Devine finally took place. This was the seventh and last to be performed by the Reverend Harold Wanger. John Devine's five fellow poker-players had already been laid to rest, as had the unfortunate young deputy, Larry Paulson.

There was an impressive turn-out. Harvey Littlejohn, the new mayor of Faro's Creek, Marshal Jim Niven and Doc Bailey were amongst those attending, as were several of Burkeville's most prominent citizens and various of Burke County's ranchers and homesteaders.

A solemn-faced Sheriff Donnie Dykes greeted Will Devine.

'A sad day, Will,' he said glumly. 'An' it seems we let that murderin' sonofabitch, Luis Bucca, git clean away.'

'Mebbe. Mebbe not,' said Devine.

'What are yuh sayin'?'

'Me and Jack here, we ain't given up hope that we'll catch the bastard. Have we, Jack?'

'No, sirree!' said the Kentuckian.

'Is that a fact?' The sheriff eyed each man in turn and enquired, 'You fellers gonna need any help?'

'No,' said Stone. 'I don't reckon so.'

'This is personal,' added Devine. 'We aim to bring him in an' see him dancin' at the end of a rope.'

'What about Al Moody?' asked Dykes.

'We catch Bucca, then I figure we can persuade him to name his employer,' replied Devine. 'That should be enough to convict Moody.'

'Wa'al, I wish you both luck,' said the sheriff.

'Thanks.'

Donnie Dykes was the only person to greet Will Devine before the commencement of the funeral. Devine then took his place beside the grieving widow and her two sons, while Sarah Rennie, who had come to support him, stood a few paces away, with the Kentuckian, Jack Stone.

An emotional, yet dignified funeral service

followed and thereafter Will Devine, Chrissie and the boys were offered condolences by the various dignitaries who had attended. This took quite some time, and it was almost an hour after the conclusion of the service before they were able to leave the cemetery and head back to the Double D ranch. They were escorted by the Double D hands and followed by Sarah Rennie in a gig, while Stone brought up the rear.

The future of the ranch was discussed over luncheon in the ranch house.

'So, whaddya plan doin', Chrissie?' asked Will Devine solicitously. 'You figure you can run the ranch on your own?'

'I know I can,' she declared.

'It ain't gonna be easy.'

'I realize that, but I got me a real good bunch of hands, an' Red Sykes, our top hand, he's 'bout as competent as you can git.'

'I guess.'

'Also, John Junior an' Jeff are here to help me. Ain't you, boys?' she said.

'Sure thing, Mom,' the pair chorused enthusiastically.

Will Devine glanced doubtfully at his two young nephews.

'They're still pretty young, Chrissie,' he remarked.

'They're old enough to help out.'

'Wa'al. . . .'

'Gee, Uncle Will, I'm goin' on thirteen an' Jeff'll be twelve in December! We're almost grown up!' cried John Junior.

Will Devine laughed.

'OK,' he said. 'See how it goes. But, if you need me, I'll be more'n happy to ride over an' do what I can.'

'I know that, Will, an' I appreciate it,' said Chrissie. 'But you've got your businesses in Burkeville to tend.'

'Even so.'

'Wa'al, if we're stuck at any time, Will, I'll let you know. 'Course I will.'

'You do that, Chrissie.'

'Thank you, Will.'

'For the present, me an' Jack, we'll be stayin' over at the Happy Valley spread.'

'What for?' asked Chrissie in surprise.

'Yes, why would you wanta stop there?' enquired an equally puzzled Sarah Rennie.

' 'Course, you don't know,' said Will Devine, and he went on to explain how he, Jack Stone, Harvey Littlejohn and Sheriff Donnie Dykes had deduced that Al Moody was the man who had hired Luis Bucca to carry out the Longhorn saloon massacre. Then he told them what had happened since. 'An' so, y'see,' he concluded, 'me an' Jack are expectin' Al Moody to return, probably accompanied by Don

Pedro Gomez, to negotiate the sale of the ranch.'

'Why don't you have the sheriff an' some of his deppities join you there?' asked an anxious Chrissie.

'No, we can handle it, cain't we, Jack?'

The Kentuckian smiled.

'I reckon.'

'What . . . what if this Luis Bucca also turns up?' demanded Sarah.

'We're hopin' he will,' said Stone.

'But . . . but he's a cold-blooded killer!' cried Sarah.

'A mighty dangerous man,' added Chrissie. 'An' you're no gunman, Will.'

'Nope, but I can use one, an' Jack's 'bout the best gunfighter I ever met.'

The two women transferred their gaze to the Kentuckian. They observed the craggy features, the broken nose and the ice-cold blue eyes. Here, they concluded, was the very man to have by your side in a tight corner.

'You'll take good care that nuthin' happens to Will, won't you?' pleaded Sarah.

Stone grinned.

'I'll do my best,' he promised.

'Aw, shucks, I ain't no baby needs mollycoddlin'!' exclaimed an embarrassed Will Devine.

' 'Course not,' said Chrissie. 'But, like I jest said, you ain't no gunman neither.'

'OK! OK! We'll be careful,' promised Devine. 'You don't need to worry on that score.'

'That's right,' agreed Stone. 'We won't be takin' no unnecessary chances.'

'Satisfied?' asked Devine.

'Guess we'll have to be,' said his sister-in-law.

Sarah said nothing, but continued to look decidedly worried.

After the meal, she said that she had to be going, and Will Devine escorted her outside to her gig. Stone, Chrissie and the two boys tactfully remained indoors.

'Thank you for coming, Sarah. I sure 'preciated your support,' said Devine, as they paused beside the gig.

'Did you?'

'Yeah. It was good of you to come. I mean, you've got a roomin'-house to run, an' then there's your young son. . . .'

'I got Mary Chambers to look after both Billy an' the roomin'-house for me.'

'Even so.'

'I wanted to come, Will.'

So saying, Sarah threw her arms round Devine's neck and, standing on tiptoe, reached up and kissed him. Devine promptly responded and drew the blonde into his arms. He had thought that Sarah was not quite ready for remarriage, but now he was not so sure. Perhaps she was, after all?

132

As he released her, Devine determined to put the question just as soon as he had avenged his brother's death. He felt that that piece of unfinished business had to be concluded first. Until Al Moody and Luis Bucca were brought to justice, he could not, would not contemplate his future.

'I'll see you back in Burkeville. Soon,' he promised.

Following the departure of Sarah, Will Devine and the Kentuckian took their leave of Chrissie and her two sons and headed towards the Happy Valley ranch.

For the next few days, the pair busied themselves about the ranch, helping Bill Lawton and his men with their various jobs. While they did this, one hand was detailed to keep his eyes peeled for the return of Al Moody.

And so it was that, on the morning of their fourth day at the ranch, Harry Carey, the youngest of the Happy Valley's hands, rode up to the ranch house with the news that a lone rider was heading their way. Devine and Stone were on the stoop, proposing to ride out and brand some steers. Immediately, they mounted their horses and followed young Harry Carey to a high bluff that overlooked the trail from the south. A tiny dot in the far distance was approaching at a steady trot.

'Did you spy him from here?' demanded Devine.

The cowboy shook his head.

'No, Mr Devine. I was someways south of here. Spotted him as he passed beneath me on his way through Dickens' Pass. I was on the rim, y'see.'

'You got a good look at him?'

'I did, sir.'

'Wa'al, is it Al Moody?'

'No, sirree! Whoever he is, he's a Mexican. Leastways, he's dressed like one, wearin' a sombrero an' that kinda thing.'

'Is he dressed all in black?'

'Er ... um ... now let me think.' Harry Carey scratched his head. 'He was mostly,' he said finally. 'But I'm pretty sure he was wearin' a white shirt.'

'That don't sound like Luis Bucca,' said Devine.

'Bucca wouldn't have no reason to come here on his own,' opined Stone.

'No, I s'pose not.'

'So, let's jest wait until the feller passes beneath us, then ride down an' cut off his retreat. We can find out who he is then.'

'OK, Jack. Let's do that.'

The wait seemed eternal, although, in fact, it was only a few minutes before the Mexican rode past. Thereupon, the trio cantered down on to the plain and, riding up behind the Mexican, ordered him to halt. He promptly obliged and turned to face them.

'*Buenos dias, señors!*' he said with a broad smile. 'This is the Happy Valley ranch?'

'It is,' said Devine.

'*Buenos*! Then, you will take me to Señor Lawton, please.'

'An' who might you be, *señor*?' enquired Stone.

'I am Roberto Gomez. My father is Don Pedro, who—'

'We've heard of Don Pedro,' said Stone.

'Yes, I b'lieve he is proposin' to buy the Happy Valley spread,' remarked Devine.

'Perhaps?'

'It ain't certain?' said Devine.

'No, *señor*, it is not certain. That is why I am here.'

'To determine whether the ranch is worth buyin'?'

'*Sí señor*.' The young Mexican eyed Will Devine curiously. 'But what is this to you? Are you perhaps Señor Lawton?'

'Nope. I ain't Bill Lawton.'

'Then. . . ?'

'Let's ride on to the ranch house an' I'll explain there.'

'Yes, that is a good idea. I have ridden long and hard and should like to dismount,' said Roberto Gomez.

He turned his horse's head and continued on his way. The others followed.

Once they reached the ranch house Harry Carey rode off to carry on with his normal duties, while Devine, Stone and the young Mexican entered the house. The late Lyle Moody's housekeeper, an elderly Pueblo woman, bustled round and produced some coffee and flat-cakes, then disappeared.

'Now,' said Will Devine to the Mexican, 'let me ask you a coupla questions, an' then I'll explain what me an' my pal, Jack Stone, are doin' here.'

'Very well, *señor*,' replied Roberto Gomez.

'I take it that the feller who's proposin' to sell the Happy Valley to your father is stayin' at Don Pedro's hacienda?'

'Yes. Señor Al Moody is to remain at our hacienda until my return.'

'I see. An' who introduced Al Moody to your father?'

'My cousin.'

'Ah, your cousin! Luis Bucca, sometimes known as the Devil's Left Hand?'

'Yes.' Roberto Gomez looked a trifle uncomfortable. 'Luis brings shame to our family, but it is to be hoped that he will now renounce his life of crime.'

' 'Cause he's to have a share of whatever price Al Moody gits for the ranch?'

'Yes, he is to receive fifty per cent.'

Devine whistled softly.

'Al Moody should've paid the murderin' bastard what he owed him, 'stead of tryin' to double-cross him,' commented Stone.

'I would not know about that,' said Roberto Gomez.

136

'D'you know why Al Moody owed him?' enquired Devine.

'I believe Luis did him a favour.'

'You got any idea what kinda favour?'

'Luis is a hired gun.' Roberto Gomez looked less than happy as he spat out these words. 'I can only think that he killed some enemy of Señor Moody,' he added.

'No, that ain't quite right,' said Devine.

'No?'

'No, *señor*, it sure ain't.' Devine stared hard at the young Mexican and then went on, 'Let me put you in the picture.'

Roberto Gomez paled and his eyes expressed only too clearly the horror he felt, as Will Devine recounted the massacre at the Longhorn saloon and explained why Al Moody had thought it necessary for Luis Bucca to murder not only his brother, but all who were playing cards together on that fateful afternoon.

'Neither Al Moody nor your cousin must be allowed to profit from this crime,' growled Stone.

Robert Gomez shook his head.

'No,' he said, 'they must not. In these circumstances, my father will most certainly not purchase this ranch.'

'They must hang for what they did.'

'I agree. But why, Señor Stone, are you involved in this matter? Are you and your friend peace-officers?'

The Kentuckian smiled wryly.

'Nope.'

'Then, why. . . ?'

'My name is Will Devine and my brother was one of those playing poker with Lyle Moody,' said Devine.

'Oh, *Madre de Dios*!'

'Mr Devine an' I intend headin' for your father's hacienda, where we propose to arrest Al Moody an' your cousin,' said Stone.

'But, if you are not peace-officers. . . ?'

'That won't stop us. We'll jest make us a citizen's arrest,' said the Kentuckian.

'I see.'

'It could be that Don Pedro may object to us takin' your cousin, though?'

'No. If you tell him what you have told me, my father will make no such objection.'

'He definitely won't if you remain here.'

'What . . . what do you mean?'

'I mean, Señor Gomez, that you will be permitted to return to Mexico only after we have brought Luis Bucca back across the border.'

'This . . . this is quite unnecessary.'

'Mebbe? But we ain't takin' no chances. This way, Don Pedro is darned sure to let us take Luis Bucca. He'll want you back for certain.'

'You realize that to keep me here against my will is illegal?'

138

'Sure.'

'Sorry, Señor Gomez, but that's how it's gonna be,' said Devine.

The young Mexican grimaced, then sighed and shrugged his shoulders.

'Arrangements will be made for a coupla hands to keep a watch on you night an' day,' said Stone.

'An' you'll be confined to this here ranch house,' added Devine. 'But it'll only be for a few days, an' you'll find your stay quite comfortable.'

Again Roberto Gomez shrugged his shoulders.

'What is to be will be,' he said philosophically.

'Then let's git goin',' said Stone.

He took the young Mexican's revolver and remained with him while Devine went in search of Bill Lawton.

Devine explained matters to the foreman and, once the Mexican's horse had been stabled and two of the hands placed on guard duty at the ranch house, he was ready to leave.

'We'll be back as soon as we can,' he informed Lawton.

'You can depend on that,' said Stone.

So saying, he and Will Devine mounted their horses and headed across the plain towards the trail that would lead them south into Mexico.

TEN

The two men rode at a gallop, for they were anxious to reach their destination and bring Al Moody and his murderous associate to justice. Consequently, only three days after leaving the Happy Valley ranch, they forded the Pecos River and crossed over into the Coahuila province of Mexico.

Their eventual arrival at the hacienda of Don Pedro Gomez was on a bright August morning. They were no more than a quarter of a mile inside its boundary when they were spotted by one of his *vaqueros*. By the time they had proceeded a further half-mile, they found themselves surrounded by half a dozen of his people.

The leader of the *vaqueros* was Don Pedro's youngest son, Raimundo. He addressed the two Americans.

'This is not open range,' he said stiffly. 'This land is owned by my father, Don Pedro Gomez.'

'Yeah, we're aware of that,' retorted Jack Stone.

'You have business with my father?' Raimundo looked sceptical.

'We ain't rustlers, if that's what you're thinkin'.'

'No?'

'Nope.'

'Then, perhaps you will tell me what manner of business you have with my father?'

'It concerns a certain Al Moody an' his dealin's with your cousin. Luis Bucca.'

Raimundo Gomez studied the two strangers closely.

'You are not friends of Señor Moody?' he said perceptively.

'We sure ain't,' agreed Stone.

'Well, then, we shall escort you to my father's ranch house.'

'Thanks.'

'Yeah. Thank you, Señor Gomez,' added Will Devine.

So large was Don Pedro's hacienda that it was late afternoon before the cavalcade eventually drew up in front of the ranch house. Don Pedro and his two guests had been sitting on the veranda enjoying a siesta after a lengthy luncheon. Luis Bucca was the first to be wakened by the sound of the approaching hoof-beats. The horsemen were still some way off and indistinct in the shimmering heat, but Bucca's instincts told him that there was trouble coming.

He therefore slipped quickly inside the house. Crouching next to one of its open windows, he was able to observe and listen to all that passed outside. Don Pedro and Al Moody, meantime, had also wakened and risen, ready to greet their visitors.

'These men say that they have business with you, Father,' explained Raimundo.

'Indeed?'

'Yes, Don Pedro. My name is Will Devine and this is my friend, Jack Stone,' said Devine.

'Well, you had better dismount, gentlemen,' said Don Pedro. 'Come, join us on the veranda. You, too, Raimundo.'

'Yes, Father.'

The three dismounted, while the five *vaqueros* wheeled round and sped off, back out on to the range. They had work to do and knew that, had Don Pedro wanted them to stay, he would have ordered them to do so.

Once he, his son and the others had settled themselves upon the veranda, Don Pedro addressed the newcomers.

'I would order refreshments, but I think it best we discuss your business first,' he said.

Al Moody recognized Will Devine and, recalling that John Devine was one of Luis Bucca's victims at the Longhorn Saloon, he felt suddenly ill at ease.

'You keep poor company,' remarked Devine.

'I beg your pardon?'

'I refer to that sonofabitch sittin' next to you. Don Pedro.' And, when Don Pedro glanced to his right, he added, 'Yeah, that there snake in the grass, Al Moody.'

'Now, lookee here—' began Moody.

'Shuddup!' said Stone and, although the Kentuckian's tone was quiet, the look in his eye effectively silenced the saloonkeeper.

'Perhaps you will be so kind as to explain why you refer to Señor Moody so disparagingly?' said Don Pedro.

'I b'lieve he's here hopin' to sell you the Happy Valley ranch?' said Devine.

'That is correct.'

'Hell, there ain't nuthin' wrong with that!' exclaimed Moody. 'I inherited it from my brother Lyle, an' since I ain't cut out to be no rancher I figured—'

'Have you told Don Pedro how you came into this inheritance?' demanded Devine.

'No. There didn't seem no call to tell him.'

'Then I shall tell him now.'

'Proceed, Señor Devine,' said Don Pedro, his curiosity roused.

'Yes, do!' added Raimundo, for he, too, sensed that the revelation would be dramatic.

'Al Moody was in cahoots with your nephew, Luis Bucca. Indeed, I'd expected to find both of 'em here,' said Devine.

143

Don Pedro glanced about him. Where was Luis? He had been sitting with them on the veranda only minutes earlier. But he decided to say nothing until he had heard what Will Devine had to say.

'Please proceed,' he said.

'Moody's business-venture up north looks doomed. He owns a saloon in a cow town named Lynx Crossing, a town that's well on its way to becomin' a ghost town. So, he had a bright idea. He figured that if he inherited the Happy Valley ranch, he could well sell it for a price that'd set him up for the rest of his life. 'Course, he could only do so should the current owner, his brother Lyle, die.'

'Do you mean. . . ?'

'Yes, Don Pedro, he hired your nephew to assassinate his brother.'

Don Pedro gasped.

'So, that is the service Luis performed for you!' he said, turning and glaring angrily at the saloon-keeper.

'You didn't know?' said Stone.

'I did not. I should have asked, but I preferred not to know what my nephew had done,' replied Don Pedro, adding repentantly, 'It was wrong of me.'

'Yeah, it was,' agreed Stone.

'An' that ain't all,' said Devine.

'Not all! What else could this son of Satan have asked of him?' enquired the rancher.

Devine told him.

'*Madre de Dios*!' exclaimed Don Pedro, then he asked in a low voice, 'And one of these men whom Luis killed, the one named John Devine, he was your brother?'

'Yeah.'

'So, y'see, Don Pedro,' explained Stone, 'me an' Will, we've come to take that there stinkin' polecat an' your murderin' nephew back to Faro's Creek.'

'Where both of 'em will hang for sure,' said Devine.

'I see.' Don Pedro looked distinctly unhappy. 'You can take Señor Moody, certainly, but—'

'You ain't gonna protect Luis Bucca, surely?' cried Devine.

'No, Father, you can't!' agreed Raimondo, who had been both shocked and sickened by what he had just heard.

'Luis is my late sister's son. I owe it to her. . . .'

'You propose to let him go, so that he can carry on murderin' innocent folks?' demanded Devine.

'Well, it is difficult for me. I. . . .'

'We figured you might play it this way,' said Stone.

'I . . . I do not understand?'

'We've ridden straight from the Happy Valley, where we spoke with the ranch foreman,' said Devine.

'So?'

'He was awaitin' Moody's return, mebbe with you in tow. Only you didn't come. But your son, Roberto, did.'

'You wanta see him again, you better hand over Bucca,' growled Stone.

'This . . . this is not right! Roberto has no part in this!' protested the rancher.

'Father is right. You cannot use my brother as a hostage!' ejaculated Raimondo.

'Oh, but we can!' said Devine.

'Mebbe it ain't legal or even fair, but that's the way it is. There ain't no way we're gonna let you protect Luis Bucca,' stated the Kentuckian.

Don Pedro eyed the two Americans. He realized that both were implacable. Also, in his heart, he knew that there was justice in their stance, albeit rough justice.

'You have not hurt Roberto?' he said anxiously.

'Nope. Your son is bein' well treated,' replied Stone.

'An' he'll be released jest as soon as Jack an' me turn up at the Happy Valley with this skunk an' your nephew,' added Devine.

'Don't . . . don't listen to 'em!' interjected a nervous Al Moody. 'They won't dare do nuthin' to Roberto.'

'No?'

'No. You . . . you needn't git involved. Jest keep these two here for a coupla hours while Luis an' me

146

make our escape. Then let 'em come after us. We'll take our chances from then on.'

'Excuse me, Don Pedro,' said Will Devine before the rancher could reply.

He rose from his chair and stepped across to where Al Moody was sitting. Then, leaning over the saloonkeeper, he dragged him bodily out of his chair and drove his left fist hard into the other's belly. Moody gasped and doubled up. Immediately, Devine's right fist smashed into his jaw and lifted him clean off his feet. Moody crashed back against the wall of the ranch house, then, as he tottered forward, Devine struck him with another two tremendous blows. The first smashed his nose to a pulp and the second knocked out half a dozen of his teeth. Moody sank to the floor unconscious, where Devine proceeded to stave in his ribs with a series of well-aimed kicks.

Eventually Raimundo and the Kentuckian stepped in and pulled him off the saloonkeeper.

'Easy, Will, easy,' said Stone. 'Let it be.'

'Yes, señor. If you do not stop, you will kill him,' counselled Raimundo.

'Which would be a pity,' said Stone, 'for that'd be lettin' the sonofabitch off easy.'

Devine nodded, breathing heavily and still shaking with rage. Presently, he calmed down and Stone and the young Mexican felt it was safe to release him.

'I ... I'm sorry, Jack. Guess I lost my temper. Listenin' to Moody tryin' to talk Don Pedro into lettin' him go, it was jest too much,' explained Devine.

'It was understandable,' said Don Pedro.

'Sure was,' agreed Stone.

'So, where do we go from here?' Devine demanded of the rancher.

Don Pedro sighed and shrugged his shoulders.

'I will not stand in your way,' he stated. 'You may take both Señor Moody and my nephew back across the border to stand trial.'

Devine glanced at the senseless saloonkeeper and smiled wryly.

'Don't figure he'll give us much trouble,' he commented.

'Nope. But where in tarnation is Bucca?' asked Stone.

'My nephew was here only a few minutes before you rode in,' said Don Pedro. 'We had lunched rather too well and Señor Moody and I must have fallen asleep. When your arrival woke us, Luis was no longer sitting on the veranda.'

'So, where the hell is he?' Devine repeated the Kentuckian's question.

All four looked about them. There were several outhouses, cabins and stables where he could be hiding. Ahead of them, the plain was empty except for a few head of cattle in the distance.

'We had best make a search of the buildings,' suggested Don Pedro.

While he was speaking, Raimundo slipped inside the ranch house. Then, before any of the others had proceeded more than a few yards, he reappeared, accompanied by his mother.

'You will be wasting your time!' he cried.

The three returned to the foot of the steps leading up to the veranda.

'What do you mean?' demanded Don Pedro.

'Tell Father,' said Raimundo.

Don Pedro's wife, Maria, broke into a torrent of Spanish. Then, once she had finished, Don Pedro turned to his guests.

'All the time were talking,' he said, 'Luis was listening inside the house.'

'Holy cow!' cried Stone.

'He took advantage of Señor Devine's assault upon Señor Moody to leave by the back door, mount his horse and ride off.'

'He is headed for the Serranias del Burro,' added Raimundo.

'Once Luis reaches those mountains you will have little or no chance of finding him,' remarked Don Pedro.

'Don't you believe it,' retorted Devine.

'I beg your pardon?'

'Jack here is 'bout as good a tracker as you'll git.'

'That's somethin' of an exaggeration, Will,' said

149

Stone, with a smile. 'But I was taught by a Kiowa Injun an' served several years as an Army scout, so, though I say it myself, I ain't too bad.'

'Pretty darned good, I'd say,' declared Devine.

'You will follow my nephew into the mountains?' enquired Don Pedro.

'Yup,' said Stone.

'I'll ride with you,' stated Devine. 'I think we can trust Don Pedro to make sure Al Moody stays put.'

'No. You stay here an' take care of Moody,' said Stone.

'But, Jack—'

'No buts, Will. Trackin' Bucca won't be easy. I'll be best on my own.'

'Wa'al, if'n you're sure?'

'I am, Will.'

Devine nodded, He desperately wanted to catch up with Luis Bucca, yet he realized his limitations and had no wish to hinder the Kentuckian and, in so doing, give the Mexican a chance to escape. Therefore, he would do as Stone suggested, albeit reluctantly.

'You'll do nuthin' to prevent Jack catchin' your nephew?' he enquired of the rancher.

Don Pedro smiled sadly.

'No,' he said. 'And you are welcome to stay here as my guest. Together, we shall ensure that Señor Moody goes nowhere.'

'An' when Jack returns with Bucca, you'll let us

take him an' Moody back across the border?'

'You have my word.'

Devine believed him. After all, Don Pedro presumably wanted to see his son, Roberto, again.

'I'll be goin', then,' said Stone.

'Good luck!'

'*Muchisima suerte*!' cried Raimundo.

They watched the Kentuckian mount his bay gelding and ride off. Then, as they climbed up onto the veranda, Don Pedro clapped Will Devine on the shoulder.

'It is as well you are holding Roberto,' he confessed, 'for it means that I must do the right thing. How my sainted sister could have borne such a son as Luis, I do not understand. He is aptly named the Devil's Left Hand.'

'That he is,' agreed Devine heartily.

They bent down to tend to Al Moody, who by now was groaning and showing signs of recovering his senses.

Jack Stone, meantime, was riding hell for leather towards the distant mountains. He had ridden through the Serranias del Burro some years earlier when in pursuit of a band of renegade Indians who had fled across the border from Texas. He could not claim an intimate knowledge of the region, however. Nevertheless, he was determined that Luis Bucca should not escape him. He would pick up the shootist's trail and hunt him down. After all, Bucca was a gunslinger, not a mountain man. For him the Serranias del Burro would be hostile terrain.

In this assessment of the Devil's Left Hand, Stone was correct. Luis Bucca did not relish the ride through that arid, inhospitable territory. Both in Mexico and across the border in the United States, he was a frequenter of saloons, cantinas, bordellos, theatres and dance halls. The song, 'Cigareets an' whiskey, an' wild, wild women', could have been written specially for him. At home at a card-table or in some sporting woman's boudoir, Bucca usually kept strictly to well-marked trails when travelling between towns. He was a town dweller with no great love of the outdoors.

As he wound his way up into the mountains through rocky ravines and narrow, steep-sided gorges, the Mexican reflected on his situation. How many men had he killed during the course of his career as a professional assassin? Twenty, thirty, forty maybe? He had lost count, yet he had not lost his desire to kill. Killing had become a drug. It was his *raison d'être*, and he was quite clear who his next victim would be. Al Moody had double-crossed him and now there was no chance that the saloonkeeper would pay him his fee. Therefore, Moody must die. But, firstly, Bucca needed to shake off any pursuers.

Ahead of him stood one of the many mesas of the Serranias del Burro and Bucca observed that a narrow path wound its way to the top. He urged his black mare forward and upward. The sure-footed animal clattered up the rock-strewn path, her rider pale-faced and trembling, his eyes averted so that he should not see the path's edge and the sheer drop below. Slowly, steadily, he continued to climb until at last he reached the mesa's wide, flat summit. From this eminence, he could look back and scan the trail behind him.

A little time passed, then Bucca spotted the lone pursuer. The horseman crossed a long, wide, scree-covered slope and vanished into the rocky ravine from which Bucca had recently emerged. Bucca grinned and dismounted. Al Moody would not, after all, be his next victim. He pulled his Winchester from the saddle boot and, finding a convenient boulder on which to rest the rifle, he settled down to wait. When his pursuer appeared from the mouth of the ravine and reached the foot of the mesa, he would prove an easy target and Bucca would shoot him dead. Then, as there seemed to be no other pursuers, the Mexican would be safe to proceed on his way and, in due time, exact his revenge upon Al Moody.

But Luis Bucca did not know either the identity or the calibre of the man pursuing him. Jack Stone had quickly picked up Bucca's tracks and, keeping his eyes peeled as he rode deep into the mountains, had observed the Mexican ride up on to the mesa.

Smiling grimly, the Kentuckian had watched as

Bucca settled down, then he had ridden, as Bucca expected him to do, into the mouth of the ravine. He knew that, upon emerging from the far end, he would present Bucca with a perfect shot. Consequently, he had no intention of riding out on to the open ground that surrounded the mesa. He had a quite different plan.

As he trotted through the ravine, Stone carefully scanned both sides. Its steep, perpendicular walls towered upwards to his left and to his right. His plan, to climb to the rim and so put himself on a level with the summit of the mesa, was, he concluded, impossible. He cursed beneath his breath.

What would he do? He was fast approaching the far end of the ravine. Just before the Kentuckian reached it, he spotted two tumbles of large boulders, one on either side of the trail. Upon coming abreast of them, he quickly dismounted and grabbed the rifle from his saddle boot. Then, he led the gelding into the left-hand tumble of rocks and hobbled the horse there so that only its head, shoulders and back could be seen from the trail. From there he hurried across to the opposite tumble of rocks and swiftly dropped out of sight.

It was high noon and a remorseless sun beat down from the cloudless blue sky. Stone was glad to crouch in amongst the boulders, protected from both its direct heat and its intense glare. All he could do now was watch and wait. Eventually, the Mexican would have to come down from the mesa. From his hiding place Stone could see its base and the spot where the path up to the summit began. This, he concluded, was just out of rifle range. In consequence, should Luis Bucca descend, then decide to continue on his way into the mountains, Stone would be unable to prevent him from doing so. He would simply have to mount up and resume his pursuit of the assassin.

However, Stone reckoned that Bucca's curiosity would get the better of him, that he would be puzzled by Stone's non-appearance from the mouth of the ravine and would want to investigate before proceeding any further. And if he did. . . ? Stone permitted himself a quiet smile.

Meanwhile, up on top of the mesa, Luis Bucca was indeed puzzled. He was convinced that the rider he had spotted was, in fact, pursuing him. And he could not understand why this pursuer had not yet emerged from the ravine. The minutes ticked slowly past. When a whole hour had elapsed since the lone rider could reasonably have been expected to appear, Bucca's patience ran out.

The Mexican rode back down the winding path to the foot of the mesa. Which way? Common sense decreed that he should carry straight on into the mountains. To do otherwise would be to take an almighty and unnecessary risk. Yet, just as Stone suspected, Bucca's curiosity had been roused and he felt obliged to satisfy it, despite the risk involved.

Throwing caution to the winds, the Mexican rode at full gallop towards the mouth of the ravine. As he entered it, he straight away observed Stone's bay gelding in the midst of the boulders to his right. Immediately he reined in the mare and pulled the pearl-handled British Tranter from its holster.

Behind Bucca, Stone rose from his hiding place and promptly shot him, aiming for and hitting him in the left shoulder. The .44 calibre slug smashed Bucca's shoulder-blade, and the force of it sent him forward, out of the saddle and crashing to the ground. Bucca hit the dirt with a thud and, before he could recover, Stone was on top of him.

The Kentuckian scooped up the British Tranter, which had fallen from Bucca's grasp, and hurled it thirty yards away down the trail. At the same time, he rammed the barrel of his Frontier Model Colt hard into the back of the Mexican's skull.

'Got you, you sonofabitch!' he growled.

It took some moments before Bucca could regain his breath. When he did so, he gasped, 'So, you have got me. What do you intend doing? Will you kill me, perhaps?'

'Oh, no! You don't git off that easy,' retorted Stone.

'What . . . what do you mean?'

'I'm takin' you back to Texas. You sure ain't gonna cheat the hangman.'

'It is a long way back to Texas, *señor.*'

'Don't worry, I'll git you there.'

'Perhaps?'

'Definitely.'

So saying, Stone quickly removed the gun from the back of Bucca's skull, reversed it and struck the Mexican a tremendous blow with the butt. Bucca grunted and slumped forward on to his face.

Stone gazed down at the senseless Mexican, smiled broadly and slowly dropped the Frontier Model Colt into its holster. Then he began to prepare Bucca for the ride back to Don Pedro Gomez's hacienda.

First, he tore Bucca's shirt from his back and fashioned it into a makeshift bandage to stanch the flow of blood from Bucca's shoulder wound. Second, he lifted the Mexican into his arms and draped him across the saddle of his black mare. This done, he tied Bucca's wrists and ankles with some cord from his saddle-bag and, using the remainder of the cord, strapped him securely on to the saddle.

Next, Stone mounted his bay gelding and then, leading the mare by her bridle, the Kentuckian began the return journey.

The ride passed without incident, although Luis Bucca recovered consciousness half-way between the ravine and their destination and spent the rest of the journey swearing in Spanish at his captor.

Presently, late in the afternoon, the pair crossed

the boundary of Don Pedro's hacienda, where they were spotted by a couple of Don Pedro's *vaqueros* and escorted to the ranch house.

There they were met by the rancher, his sons, Ricardo and Raimundo, Will Devine and a sullen-faced Al Moody.

'Ah, so you have captured my nephew!' exclaimed Don Pedro.

'Yup,' replied Stone.

'Release me, Uncle!' cried Bucca. 'You cannot let these gringos take me.'

'You are a disgrace to my family,' Don Pedro cut him short. 'You will go with the *Americanos* to be tried and punished for what you have done.'

'But, Uncle—'

'Silence!' Don Pedro turned to face Stone. 'Untie him, please, *señor*. His wound needs tending, if you are to get him to Texas alive. Also, before you set out, you all must eat.'

And so it was settled. Don Pedro's wife cleansed and rebound the wound with fresh bandages. Then, when they had all eaten at Don Pedro's table, Stone tied both Luis Bucca's and Al Moody's wrists together. He and Will Devine helped the two miscreants climb into the saddle and promptly mounted themselves. And when Stone turned to bid Don Pedro farewell, he found that the rancher's sons had also mounted their horses.

'Ricardo and Raimundo will ride with you,' Don

Pedro informed him.

'Wa'al, I dunno 'bout that?'

'I must insist.'

'But—'

'Your journey will take several days and nights, yes?'

'Yeah.'

'So, from time to time, you will need to rest. Then Ricardo and Raimundo can take their turn in guarding your prisoners.'

'Wa'al. . . .'

'That makes sense, Jack,' said Will Devine.

'I s'pose.'

'Also, they will be company for Roberto on his journey home,' added the rancher.

Stone mused for a moment or two, then nodded.

'OK,' he said. 'I guess your sons are welcome to join us, Don Pedro.'

'Then, I bid you *adios, amigos,*' stated Don Pedro.

'So long, an' thanks for your hospitality,' said Stone.

'Yeah, thanks a lot,' added Devine wholeheartedly.

Thereupon, the small cavalcade wheeled round and, led by the big Kentuckian, headed northwards, away from the ranch house and off in the direction of the border. Don Pedro watched them go. A man of honour, he could not deny that his nephew had become a cold-blooded killer and should face the consequences of his actions. Therefore, he had allowed the two Americans to take him with them, in the sure knowledge that he would hang. But this had not been easy for him. After all, Luis Bucca was his late sister's son.

The rancher waited until Jack Stone and the others were mere dots in the distance. Then he turned and walked slowly round behind the ranch house. He passed through a small flower-garden to the family cemetery.

There were two recent graves. One held Don Pedro's mother and the other his sister.

It was here that he silently prayed and begged his sister's forgiveness for what he had just done. He reflected sorrowfully that Luis Bucca had been born one of God's children, yet would assuredly die as the Devil's Left Hand.